MORE THAN ANYTHING

MORE THAN ANYTHING 1

TT KOVE

ARCTIC CIRCLE PRESS

More Than Anything © TT Kove

Published by Arctic Circle Press

This book is a work of fiction and as such all characters and situations are fictitious. Any resemblance to actual people, place, or events is coincidental.

More Than Anything is set in Norway, and as such uses British English throughout.

PART I
THIS IS HOW OUR STORY BEGAN

JØRGEN

CHAPTER 1

I'd just made sure my car was locked when I saw him.

He stood on the pavement, right next to the gate to my flat. He was properly bundled up for winter, so he shouldn't have caught my attention at all, aside from the fact he was in front of my gate. But the blank expression on his young face, *that* did catch my attention.

I pocketed my keys and walked slowly towards him. I didn't want to startle him, but at the same time that blank look had me worried.

"Hey. Are you all right?" I spoke loud enough to catch the attention of someone standing only a foot away, but he didn't react at all.

Frowning, I stepped closer. *Is he drunk?* I didn't

think so. Drunkenness would have him stumbling around, not standing perfectly still. Maybe he was high on something? That was more difficult to determine, though.

"Are you all right?"

I tried again now that I was closer to him. There was still no reaction, and I was really starting to worry. I tapped a finger against my thigh and wondered if I should call for an ambulance when he suddenly jerked and fell to the ground. His body spasmed, and it took me a couple of seconds to realise that he was having an epileptic seizure.

I crouched down next to him, grateful for all the snow piled up on the pavement that softened his fall. His entire body seized violently and his lips turned slightly blue. I didn't try to touch him or hold him. I'd dealt with epileptic seizures before, though that was a part of my past I shied away from. My knowledge came in handy now, however. If I hadn't been familiar with epilepsy, I might've freaked out, but I'd seen this several times before. Granted, it had been years, but it wasn't exactly something I'd forget.

The seizure didn't last more than a few minutes, definitely less than five, so I figured he was good when another one didn't start. But he was still in no condition to go anywhere. His eyes had closed and his breathing was turning deep. He was falling asleep.

"Fuck." I glanced around. I wasn't sure why I did it; it had been obvious earlier that he was alone.

If anyone had been there, they wouldn't have been able to do anything anyway. So I did the only responsible thing I could and hefted him up in my arms. He was young and wearing a rucksack.

I managed to get him inside without dropping him. Not that he was particularly heavy, but it was a bit complicated to pick up my keys and unlock the door when my arms were busy holding him. It was also awkward thanks to the thick, slippery jacket he was wearing, and the heavy rucksack.

My flat only had one bedroom, so that was where I put him down. Right in the middle of my own bed. I hadn't made it that morning, and it was a mess, but the kid was already asleep. I supposed it didn't really matter. I took off the rucksack and jacket before carefully laying him back down again. His trousers were clean, only slightly damp from the snow, which meant he hadn't pissed himself during the seizure. I pulled off his Converse last before I tucked my duvet over him. He was in all of his clothes, but I'd left my window open and the room was freezing.

I closed the window on my way out then deposited his shoes and jacket in the hallway. The rucksack I took with me into the living room, where I promptly started rifling through the contents. I probably should have felt guilty, but the kid had just had a seizure in front of me and I'd saved him from freezing to death out in the snow. I figured I was allowed some leeway.

He had a few schoolbooks in there, and I assumed from their titles he was studying Design, Arts and Craft. He was in upper secondary school, then, at least fifteen. I found a wallet next, where he had a debit card stashed inside. Geir Berger. And he was sixteen years old. Seventeen in little over a month.

I pulled out a sketchbook. It was entirely out of curiosity that I opened it. There couldn't be anything of importance in it, but I was honest enough to admit to myself that I wanted to see if he was any good. There were regular sketches of fruit and other objects, probably what he had to do in school, but there were also landscape sketches and some of people. He *was* good. I hadn't expected it. I didn't know why I hadn't, seeing as I didn't know him.

I closed the sketchbook and put it atop the rest of his books. The only thing left in the main compartment of the rucksack was a pencil case. That was of little interest. I zipped up the smaller compartment in the front and found his epilepsy medication as well as a mobile. The last one was what I'd been looking for.

It was on, and thankfully didn't have a passcode, so I could freely browse through his contacts. There was a Dad in there, but no Mum. I tried calling Dad, but was promptly told his mobile was shut off. I tried the home number too, but that just kept ringing without anyone answering.

Seemed I was stuck with the kid. What was I supposed to do with him? He could sleep all through the night from a seizure. I didn't have to go to work in the morning, it being a weekend and all, but I would need to sleep at some point. The sofa wasn't exactly a comfortable place to sleep. It wasn't even comfortable to sit on.

It was still only four in the afternoon. Maybe the father would ring once he turned his mobile on or came home to find his son gone. In the meantime, I could make myself some dinner.

I wasn't what could be called a good cook, but I managed by using a lot of canned food and bagged sauces and pasta or rice. I didn't have the skill or patience to make a proper dinner with potatoes from scratch, and I wasn't really in the mood for pasta or rice either—so I ended up frying up a simple meal of eggs and bacon. I buttered bread while it fried in the pan, then topped it all with ketchup when it was all done. It wasn't really a *dinner*, more like breakfast or supper, but it was food. Warm food, even. More than good enough.

My mobile startled me when it rang after I'd cleaned off my plate. I'd been so set on Geir's mobile ringing from the living room that I hadn't even given a thought to my own, resting in my jeans pocket.

I answered without looking at the screen first. "Yeah?"

Tarjei's laughing voice sounded in my ear. "Is that a way to greet your best mate?"

"What do you want?" I'd just seen him at work. Whatever he had to say, he could've said there. He *was* my best mate and I loved him, but after a week at work I needed some alone time. I wasn't very fond of people, after all, which he knew.

"Just wondered if you wanted to join me down at the pub?"

"No." Even the thought of it made my skin crawl. Yeah, it was definitely time for some alone time. Except I wasn't completely alone. I walked over to my bedroom and peered inside at Geir, asleep in my bed.

"Hey, at least I asked. I don't want anyone calling me a bad friend. Your loss, though." Tarjei didn't sound disappointed, but then I didn't think he had that feeling in his repertoire. He was eerily cheery at times, not to mention optimistic. He was always happy, which was the creepiest thing of all. Who was happy all the time? I wasn't even happy half the time.

"I appreciate it, mate." I tried to sound appreciative, but I wasn't sure if I managed it. I was tired after a full week of work, and dealing with people, and now I had an epileptic kid in my flat I didn't know what to do with. "I'm crashing early."

"Well, you enjoy your bed while I'll be out having fun." With that, Tarjei hung up on me. It didn't really faze me. It was typical behaviour for him, and it wasn't like I minded getting off the mobile. I wasn't a big fan of the thing.

I looked over at Geir again. He was sleeping peacefully, his head tilted towards me, and I found myself noticing the blond hair sticking up in the back where he'd been moving around in his sleep. It fell into his face in the front. He had long lashes, darker than his hair. His nose was pert with a scattering of freckles over it. He was cute, I could admit that much. But he was young, too. Way too young.

I strode back over to the sofa and spent the next few hours browsing through the telly. There wasn't anything happening on Geir's mobile, and my frown deepened each time I cast a look at it. I was grumpy, I was tired, and the sofa was hurting my backside. I wanted my bed.

It was a double, a 1.80, so there would definitely be enough space in it. But I wouldn't take kindly to waking up in bed with a stranger, so how could I do that to a kid?

The more time went by, though, the longer the mobile was silent, the less I cared. In the end, when I couldn't do anything but yawn every few minutes, I said fuck it all and went to bed. I changed into more comfortable clothes, putting on bottoms and a T-shirt so I wouldn't completely freak the kid out. Not that I slept naked, but I usually preferred to sleep bare-chested. I got hot when I slept.

Geir slept on as I slid in opposite him and made myself comfortable. I looked at him for a moment, then turned my back on him. I lay as far over on my side as I could without tumbling off the bed. I wasn't sure it was enough, but it had to do, because I was tired and he was hogging my bed, and I damn well deserved some sleep after taking him in.

I didn't exactly have a restful sleep. Every time he moved, I woke up. I'd always been a light sleeper, kind of had to be with my childhood, and it was impossible to get a good night's sleep if I shared my bed with anyone. That was why I never did. So it was a restless night, with me dozing off between his movements.

When his breathing changed from deep sleep to shallow, confused breaths, I was instantly awake. I still lay with my back to him, but now I had a dilemma to face. He would be confused, and he was waking up in a bed with another bloke. I should've got up earlier, so I would be somewhere else in the flat by the time he woke, but I had not done that, and now... well, now he was awake.

His head kept rolling from side to side. Maybe he was on the verge of panic. I pushed myself up to sit on the edge of my bed. I glanced over my shoulder at him and found wide, startlingly green eyes looking back at me.

"Hey." I greeted him in a low voice. Rubbing a hand over my face, I wondered what else to say. I wasn't good at talking to people, never had been, but it hadn't bothered me before because I simply didn't much care for people in general. This kid, however... it did bother me now that I didn't know what to say.

He blinked dazedly at me, and then his gaze fell down my body before flickering away.

"You had a seizure yesterday." I scrubbed my hand through my hair next. It felt a mess with the wax from the day before, and it must certainly look a mess as well. "I didn't know what to do with you, so

I just brought you inside." I shrugged awkwardly. This could potentially get me in trouble, if he thought there was more to it than me simply wanting to help him.

"Umm." He glanced up at me again for a brief moment, then down at himself. "Did I…?"

"No." I shook my head, knowing exactly what he was afraid of. I could only imagine how it must feel. Being subjected to epileptic seizure in itself must suck, but when said seizure could fuck up your bladder control, it couldn't be fun. In fact, I'd imagine it must be pretty mortifying. "You didn't."

He looked at me again, and his gaze was much more alert this time around. "You know about epilepsy?"

I nodded. "Someone I used to know once had it."

It wasn't the truth, but it wasn't a *lie* either. I didn't want to think about it, though, so I shoved it away as I pushed off the bed.

"Do you want breakfast?" I asked, wanting to divert the subject over to something safe. "I don't really have much in way of food, but I could run down to the bakery around the corner."

He shook his head.

"You've been asleep almost fourteen hours, you need food." I stared down at him, not backing down.

He probably hadn't eaten since lunch, if he'd been

at school. Around eleven-thirty. His gaze fell, but he nodded jerkily.

"Make yourself at home," I told him quietly. "Please don't run off." I don't know why I said that. I never would've said it to anyone else. Maybe I did because I was worried about him. He'd had a seizure, and he hadn't eaten in a very long time, and that was bad for an epileptic. They needed proper food at regular times.

I stopped by the bathroom to brush my teeth and throw some water in my face and hair. Rubbing at the day-old wax, getting most of it out, I scrubbed my hair dry with a towel. I'd just go out in my jogging trousers, the ones I'd slept in.

It wasn't like there was anyone I wanted to impress out there, as I was just skipping out for food.

It would have to do.

CHAPTER 2

I realised, once I stepped foot inside the bakery, that I hadn't asked what he liked to eat. I could simply buy bread, but then I didn't have anything to have on it besides eggs. Making a quick decision, not wanting to stay longer than possible, I bought two pizza toasts and two pasta salads. He had to like at least one of them. I liked both, anyway.

He was up and about when I got back home. Well, not about. He was perched tentatively on the sofa, looking at his rucksack and the mobile I'd left lying on the table the night before.

"I tried calling your dad last night," I explained to him. "His mobile was off, though, and no one answered at your landline, so…" I shrugged, not knowing what to say. I'd tried to reach his dad, but when I couldn't get a hold of him, I decided to simply let Geir be. It wasn't like he'd been bothering me.

"My dad works off-shore." He looked up at me, and once again I couldn't help but be startled at the sheer brilliance of those green eyes. It was eerie. "He's out now, and generally keeps his mobile off. He calls me every couple of days from the platform, but other than that…" It was his turn to shrug.

That explained why I hadn't got hold of the dad. "So he lets you stay here all by yourself?" I sat down next to him on the sofa and put my purchases on the table. "I forgot to ask you what you liked, so I just got something I like. I hope you like it too." I put one bag of pizza toast and one bag of pasta salad in front of him.

"I have other family. They check in with me pretty often too, if I don't contact them first. They only live a few streets from my house." He peered inside both bags. He pulled out the pizza toast, which was what I'd started with as well. It wasn't any good if it was cold, after all.

I frowned. "Is it wise to leave a kid with epilepsy on his own for weeks at a time?" I wasn't very familiar with working off-shore, but I knew those who did spent more weeks away than they did at home.

He glanced at me. "I don't have seizures very often," he said. "I just… I guess I've forgot to take my pills sometimes lately."

My frown deepened. "That's asking for trouble."

He ducked his head. "I know. I just… I forget sometimes."

"You shouldn't do that." It wasn't my place to lecture him, but I sure had to say something. "It'll only make the seizures happen more often. And make them worse."

"I know." His head was still bent, but I found my eyes drawn to his profile. He had a nice profile. Small, pert nose, pale, smooth skin, finely shaped jaw and chin, and his neck… I shook my head and looked back down at my food. He was *sixteen years old*. I should *not* look at him. There were six years between us. It wasn't all that much, but he was underage.

"Eat your food," I told him, not knowing what else to say. I wasn't very good at conversation with friends, and now there I was with a strange kid. One that I found attractive, at that.

I finished both my toast and salad, while he only barely finished the toast. "Don't you like the salad?" I asked.

"I do, it's just…" His gaze flickered to me and we

stared at each other for several moments. "I'm full. Thank you." Well, he was polite, for sure.

"Save it for dinner, then," I told him, once again making me the focus of his wide-eyed stare. "Do you have to make your dinners yourself, when your dad's not home?" Since there had been no Mum saved on his mobile, I could only reckon he had to.

He nodded. "Yeah. Though most days I go over to my uncle's house and eat there."

"Good." I couldn't help but question the fact that he was left all by himself for weeks at a time while his dad was absent. Yes, he had family that checked in on him, but he had *epilepsy*. I didn't know how severely or how often he had seizures, but if he forgot his medicine and didn't eat properly, it fucked up seizure control. I had seen it so many times when I was only a kid.

"Umm." He was looking at me again. "Thank you for taking care of me yesterday. F-for letting me sleep here, in your bed. And th-thanks for breakfast." He looked a bit flustered, and I realised the sudden stuttering was from embarrassment.

"You don't have to thank me. I couldn't very well have left you out there to freeze. It's what any decent person would do." I didn't think anyone had ever called me decent, but there was a first time for anything.

He laughed at that, but it was a bitter sound. "No, it's not. Most people at school laugh when I have a seizure."

I tensed up. "It's not funny." The cruelty of kids was sometimes stunning. I really shouldn't have been surprised; it wasn't like I'd had an easy time of it back when I was younger. But that was more thanks to adults, though my fellow schoolmates hadn't really given a shit either.

"It's not funny at all." He bowed his head again. "But they still do it every time."

"You don't have any friends, do you?" I couldn't help but stare at him again.

"No one wants to be friends with the freak who has seizures." He shook his head sadly.

"You're not a freak," I murmured. "You have a condition that you can't control."

"Tell that to all of them."

Jesus. I, at least, had Tarjei, even if no one else had given a shit. Geir had no one. Tarjei got on my nerves most of the time, but I couldn't imagine how life would've been without him. I couldn't imagine surviving my teenage years without him. He'd been there through everything.

"I'm sorry," I offered meekly, unsure of what else to say. There wasn't really anything I *could* say. There wasn't anything I could do about his situation, no matter how sad the thought of it made me.

His gaze was on me again, but I didn't look up. I didn't want him to see my face, to see what I was thinking and feeling. I was usually stone-faced, as both family and friends could attest, but I knew right now that everything was showing.

"I should go home now," he said quietly. "I have to feed my dog."

I perked up. "You have a dog?" At least he wasn't *entirely* alone when his father was gone. It made me feel better, though not a whole lot.

"I do." He nodded, a small smile finally spreading on his lips, and I couldn't help but stare at the way he seemed to light up. "He's old now, I've had him for a very long time, but he's the best dog I could've ever had. He never barks or pulls the leash. When I have seizures, he usually stays close to me until I wake up."

That did sound like a good dog. I'd never had a pet in my life, so I didn't know anything about animal behaviour, but I liked the sound of his dog. The fact that the dog stayed with him when he had seizures was very touching.

"I'll drive you," I said.

"Wha—oh no, you don't have to do that." He

stood up quickly, wringing his hands nervously. He bit his lower lip, and I watched the sight for way too long.

"I don't have to, no, but I want to." I stood up as well. I grabbed the bag with the pasta salad from the table and handed it to him. "Keep it for dinner or supper."

He stared down at it for a moment before he took it. His fingers brushed lightly over my own, and I quickly withdrew my hand once I was sure he had the bag. His fingers had been soft against my skin, and for a bloke who didn't really like being touched —I'd liked it a lot. It was disconcerting, to say the least.

We were both quiet as we left my flat and got into my car. I only asked for directions, and he only spoke to give them to me. When I'd parked outside his house, we sat for a bit in silence before he unbuckled himself. It was a small but nice-looking house, painted white with dark shutters. There was a stretch of lawn in front, a fence surrounding it.

"Thanks, again, for everything." He glanced at me, but when I met his gaze, his flickered away. He opened the car door but hesitated to get out. "Umm. I don't know your name."

"Uh." I hadn't even introduced myself? That

was... quite rude, actually, wasn't it? Considering we'd slept in the same bed the night before, and all that. "I'm Jørgen."

His gaze finally settled on me without hesitation. His lips were slightly parted, and my gaze really wanted to drop down to study them, but I forced myself to meet his eyes. I couldn't be caught staring at a sixteen-year-old's lips, no matter how tempting they were.

"I'm Geir. It was nice to meet you."

Yeah. It was actually nice to meet him too.

~

A WEEK WENT by before I saw him again.

It was more of a coincidence than anything else, because it wasn't like I'd been looking for him. I *had* been thinking about him, but that was about it.

Even when I got a job at the vocational education school, I didn't expect to see him around; while we lived in a small town, it wasn't *that* small. It wasn't like everyone knew everyone, and the school had quite a large number of students.

I'd graduated from it over four years ago, as a student on the programme for Electricity and Electronics. I'd gone the two obligatory years before I started as an apprentice electrician. I had done that simply because I'd needed to start making my own money, but I'd also taken the supplementary programme for general studies part-time. It had earned me the general university admission certification, so that if I ever did get tired of being an electrician I could apply to university. I doubted I ever would, but it was nice to have the chance.

I'd been in the basement dealing with faulty electricity in one of the buildings for hours before I took my lunch break. Not that I'd brought any lunch, as it had skipped my mind that morning, but I needed the break. I'd timed it badly, because when I got up onto the ground floor it turned out that it was the middle of the lunch break for the students as well.

I was debating between going back down into the basement and going outside for some fresh air when I heard several students, both male and female, laughing behind me. I turned, unable to contain my irritability at the high-pitched, *mocking* laughs. I didn't think they were laughing at me, but it wasn't the laughter of someone having fun with friends.

When I saw what it was they were laughing at, my temper flared. Because they were laughing at *him*. He was standing in the middle of the hall, with his head bowed and empty-handed, because all of his books were scattered around him on the floor.

"Really, Geir," one of the girls taunted, "you

should watch where you're going." It hadn't been an accident, going by the smirks on their faces. I'd seen it before, back when I was in school myself, how bullies just walked right into you on purpose, knocking books to the floor. At least they hadn't knocked *him* to the floor.

He swallowed heavily and his hands clenched and unclenched. His head was still bowed, so I couldn't see his face, but the skin I could see was flushed. He bent down slowly to gather up his books, not reacting to the continued taunts of his fellow students.

One of the blokes standing with the girl who'd spoken before stepped forward and kicked one of Geir's books away from him. He grazed Geir's hand with the kick as well, and Geir yelped as he retracted his hand and held it close to his chest.

I saw red. I strode over to pick up the book, glaring at the gathered students when I straightened up.

"Fuck off," I told them. They looked at me for a moment, seemingly startled by my sudden appearance, then scattered.

Geir lifted his head slowly, and his eyes were big as they met mine. I crouched down so we were on more of an equal level. "You should tell someone about this. I'm pretty sure the school has some anti-bullying law. If not, they *should* have one."

"Jørgen…"

My name came out in a sigh, and damn it all, but I *liked* it.

CHAPTER 3

He struggled to hold onto his books, mostly because he was holding them all at a weird angle, and I took some from him mostly to distract myself from the fact that I wanted to keep staring at him.

I stood up and helped him up on his feet as well.

Then I stood there awkwardly in front of him, still holding half of his books to my chest.

"What are you doing here?" He bit his lower lip again, and it was *distracting*.

"I'm an electrician," I said. "Got some work to do down in the basement."

He shuffled uncomfortably in front of me. "Thank you. Again. You seem to come to my rescue a lot. We shouldn't make it a habit." He chuckled, but it fell flat.

"Or maybe we should." I didn't know why I said that. All I knew was he looked uncomfortable, awkward and upset, and I just wanted to see that smile he'd given me a week ago. I liked his smile. "Maybe you need someone to come to your rescue." God, but his eyes were such a brilliant shade of green. I felt like I could lose myself in them forever.

"Are you volunteering?" The corner of his mouth tilted up into a wry smile, and I liked the daring hint to his voice.

"Maybe I am." *Is this flirting?* I'd never flirted with anyone in my entire life, but I *had* witnessed Tarjei putting on his charm on several occasions. If it was flirting, I really shouldn't have done it. He was too young, but damn it, he didn't seem to mind it at all.

He clutched tighter to his books, but his eyes never left mine. "Do you want to go outside with me? For fresh air, you know."

I nodded and we walked side by side towards the wide double doors leading outside. The snow was piled high outside, but the sun shone and several other students were scattered around the premises.

We didn't descend the stairs, only stepped out onto the landing. It was enough fresh air from there, especially as I hadn't worn my jacket. He wasn't wearing a particularly thick jacket, either.

I still holding on to a couple of his books, but his arms seemed full enough, so I continued to hold them without comment. It wasn't like I minded.

Pulling my gaze from him, I looked at the buildings surrounding us. To our right was the building where most of my classes had taken place back in the day. Opposite it was the building containing the gym and swimming pool. For a moment, I couldn't rip my attention away from it.

"So you went to this school too, didn't you?"

I pushed the bad memories back to the deepest corner of my mind. I didn't want to think about them. Thinking about them would not have left me fit to deal with other people, and I was at work. "Yeah. Yeah, I did."

"How long ago?" His shoulders were hunched up a bit, telling me clear as day that he was cold.

"Four and a half years," I muttered, and my eyes did another involuntary sweep of the premises before lingering on the gym building.

He was silent a moment. "So how old are you?"

"Twenty-two. I graduated after two years and started my apprenticeship." I cast him a small smile.

He dropped his gaze when I returned my full attention to him. He was a lot easier to look at than the buildings surrounding me and the memories associated with them.

If I'd had any choice in the matter, I wouldn't have ever gone to the school at all, but it was a job like any other, and I couldn't have very well refused it. My boss wouldn't have liked that at all. Besides, if I were to avoid every place I had a bad memory about, I wouldn't leave my front door.

"You like being an electrician?"

I shook myself out of my thoughts. I had the uncomfortable feeling that he'd been looking at me for a while, when I'd been completely submerged in my own head, and I hated when that happened. At least nothing particularly bad had surfaced, or else I'd be in a right danger of having an anxiety attack in front of him.

"I do. It's an okay job." I shrugged slightly and shifted my hold on his books.

"Did you always know you were going to be an electrician?"

"It just happened, really. I chose the course because there was a lot of maths, and well... I didn't mind it, so I finished." I shook my head.

He grimaced. "So you're good at maths, then? I hate numbers and equations and whatever."

I smiled. "Isn't that the way it tends to be when you're creative? The logical side of numbers doesn't make much sense. It doesn't matter, though, does it? Everyone's different. I, for instance, am not creative at all."

That brought the smile back to his lips as well. "I guess you're right."

"I guess so."

I could see he was shaking slightly now.

"It's cold, we should go back inside." I opened the door and held it open for him. His shoulder brushed my arm as he brushed past me. I wasn't sure if he'd done it deliberately or if it was an accident.

I COULD FEEL when the bad periods were coming. Those worse than usual, that was. The week crawled by, and by the weekend I was ready to fall into bed and never resurface.

I did crawl right into bed when I got home from work on Friday, and I stayed there until Saturday afternoon when I finally forced myself up and in the shower.

I didn't get much sleep that night. I tossed and turned, and when I finally fell asleep, I was woken by nightmares.

Several times I'd curl up in the usual position as anxiety attacks wrecked me. I was exhausted, but I knew that if I didn't get up and out, I eventually wouldn't be able to even get out of bed.

So I took a shower, got dressed, and went outside. Being outside usually helped, but not being around people, so I went for a walk. It was snowing a little and I didn't meet many people as I trudged through the streets towards the graveyard. The church stood tall and dark against the lightness of the ground and sky. Patches of the roof were covered in white, powdered snow.

There was hardly anyone about. I supposed people preferred to stay inside in the cold, especially with it being a Saturday. No work or school or other obligations to get up early for. Crossing the grave-yard slowly, I made my way up the slope leading up to the trail. I could walk the trail for hours when I felt like it, and I almost always took the long way around. Sometimes I could take the long trail several times. I buried my hands in my pockets as I reached the top of the slope and set off on mostly even ground.

The snow drifted towards the ground. It was a pretty sight, but the minuscule snowflakes were cold. At least there wasn't much wind out, or it would really have been freezing. As it was, it was perfect weather for a stroll to clear my head.

I walked past a middle-aged lady and two older

men, but otherwise it was quiet. I tried to keep my thoughts on something good, on anything but the memories that plagued me at night, but they kept resurfacing. They made my skin crawl, made me want to curl up in a corner and never resurface.

There was a bend in the trail ahead of me, and an outcropping obscured the rest of it. When I'd finally walked past, I stopped dead in my tracks.

Geir sat on one of the red benches scattered around the trail, and at his feet was a black Labrador with its head resting on his knees. Geir stroked the dog's head lovingly.

It had been a week and one day since I'd met him at the school. I hadn't seen or spoken to him since.

What were the odds that I'd actually meet him on my walk?

Pretty darn good, apparently.

I contemplated for a second turning away and walking back the way I'd come, but the simple sight of him made my skin crawl a bit less, and I found myself inexplicably drawn towards him.

"Hey." I announced my presence before approaching him any further, simply because that was what I preferred. It could end badly if people snuck up on me, but on the other hand not everyone was as broken as I was.

His head shot up and for a moment he looked

startled, maybe even a touch afraid, but he relaxed instantly once he caught sight of me. The smile he gave me then was enough to make my skin crawl in a way entirely unrelated to my nightmares and memories. It was disconcerting, but at the same time... Maybe it was good? I'd never really had anything good, so I had no idea what it was supposed to feel like.

"Hey, Jørgen." He seemed genuinely pleased to see me.

I brushed some snow away from the bench and sat down next to him. "Is this your dog?" I reached out a hand to pat the black Lab on the head and behind the ears.

"Yeah, this is Charo." Geir scratched the dog behind the other ear. "He's eleven years old now. We've had him almost my entire life. He's trained, you know, to get help when I have a seizure. He's quite intelligent."

"That's nice." I didn't know what else to say, only that I had to say *something*.

"Dad's home now. He's leaving again in a week and a half, though."

"How long does he spend at home each time?"

"Three weeks at home, three weeks off-shore."

Three weeks alone. That was a lot, wasn't it? And as he had no friends, I could only imagine how lonely he must be. It couldn't be any fun for him, suffering from epilepsy and being laughed at and taunted all the time. I couldn't even imagine what it was like. I at least had been completely ignored by my fellow classmates back when I was in school. But then my home situation had been hell enough.

His hand bumped mine, and I automatically pulled my hand back as if I'd been burned.

He looked at me, frowning in confusion. "I'm sorry."

"No, *I'm* sorry." *Seriously?* It had been something I hadn't been able to control. I didn't let people into my personal space. Not anyone. Except I probably wouldn't have minded him in it, which scared me in other ways. Still, his hand bumping mine had caused an instant reaction I hadn't been able to suppress. "I didn't mean to pull back like that. It's just... It's an automatic response to people. I'm sorry."

He drew his lower lip in-between his teeth. "It's okay." It didn't sound like it was, though.

"I mean it." I turned to look directly into his eyes. I didn't know why, but I needed him to believe me. "That's my reaction to anyone touching me. It has nothing to do with you personally."

He looked back for several seconds, and I couldn't look away—I was mesmerised by those eyes.

I shivered, and it was not at all from the cold. How could this *kid* evoke such reactions in me? He was sixteen bloody years old. He was legal, by all means, but even if he'd been closer to my own age, I was too broken. I didn't know a thing about relationships—I didn't even know if I *could* ever manage to be a part of one. I'd never wanted to before, but now, with those eyes on me... it made me want things.

It made me wish for something I'd never wished for before. Made me wish for intimacy, the good sort like I'd never experienced before, but which I saw all the time in everyone else.

"Why don't you like anyone touching you?" he asked tentatively.

I couldn't tell him. I couldn't even think about it without suffering horrible flashbacks and a subsequent anxiety attack.

"It's a long, complicated story." I hoped he'd be happy with that, because it was all I could bear to say on the subject.

At least safely, without turning into a complete wreck. I was frayed enough as it was, after the past week and the nightmares.

I couldn't deal with it.

I'd never been able to.

I didn't think I ever would be.

CHAPTER 4

A cold snout touched my hand, and I involuntarily jerked back again before I realised it was just his dog.

I stared down at his pointed black face. His eyes were big and he seemed to be begging me to touch him.

I clenched and unclenched my hands nervously. I'd never had any kind of pet before. I'd never wanted one, never been interested in any kind of animal. But that face and those eyes… they were irresistible. Kind of like Geir's.

Geir drew me in, if I wanted it or not, and now his dog turned out to have the same effect too, just in a different kind of way. I slowly reached out and petted Charo on the head. His fur was soft underneath my palm and he rubbed up closer to me.

"He likes you." Geir smiled at me. I quickly looked away. His smile was too happy, too brilliant, too stunning... It would undo me. I couldn't come undone. Too much was buried inside me.

"He's a nice dog." I looked down at him again. His tongue was hanging out now, which I supposed meant he liked being scratched behind the ears. I didn't know anything about dogs, but he wasn't moving away from me, so I was apparently doing something right.

"That he is." Geir reached out to pat the dog as well, but he didn't touch me again. Instead, he ran his hand through the soft fur on Charo's back.

His fingers were long and slim. An artist's fingers. That hand had bumped mine earlier. The skin I'd felt in that short second had been soft. It had startled me, but it had also felt... good, I supposed.

I wasn't used to being touched. I'd learned from early on that if people touched me, they hurt me. But I didn't think Geir would. He was too sweet for that. Besides, even if he did, I was bigger and broader. He didn't pose a threat to me.

Still, it was a deep-rooted reaction.

I noticed that his fingers were red. When I dared

turn my head to actually look at *him*, I saw he was huddling a bit in his jacket.

"Want to walk with me?" He was cold, and he needed to start moving. I wasn't quite feeling the cold yet, though I did feel the wind, but he was smaller than me and thus couldn't take as much as I could.

Geir nodded, a fleeting smile passed over his lips again. He stood up from the bench but leaned down to pat his dog one more time. "You're such a good dog." Charo must have been, as he didn't have a leash.

I stood up too, and we slowly continued along.

We took the long path without saying anything, headed down the slope instead of taking the even path around the outcrop. I wasn't in any hurry to be rid of his company, and he seemed he wasn't either.

It was new to me, all of it.

Besides Tarjei, no one really wanted to be around me for very long. I knew I wasn't good company. I didn't know how to make small talk. Most of the time I couldn't even get myself to shake hands with people. I certainly didn't do crowds, which was why I never went to the pub with Tarjei. He kept asking me, like the good friend he was, but I always refused. He didn't begrudge it, because he knew I had trouble dealing when surrounded by a lot of people.

"Do you come here a lot?" Geir asked, breaking the silence between us. I thought it had been a rather comfortable silence. Maybe he hadn't thought so? He seemed at ease; maybe he just really wanted to know the answer to the question.

"I guess, yeah." I looked around. The path was covered in snow now, but it would all melt soon. It was beautiful in the winter, with the snow lying heavy and colouring everything white. With the pine trees trying to hold the weight of the snow up on its branches. I liked winter. Everything was so pure. Nothing out here was dirtied. It calmed me down. Of course, I liked to walk the path in any season, but winter in particular was my favourite. "Do you?"

He nodded. "It's the easiest path to get to when I go out with Charo. And people are frequent here, if something were to happen Charo could always find someone."

I glanced at him. His lips were tilted up, but his head was downturned. He lived with the knowledge that he didn't have complete control over his own body. That he could suddenly have a seizure, anywhere he went.

It wasn't anything like me. I never worried about my health whenever I went outside. I worried more about my emotional stability. I liked to be alone, but if I did meet people I usually turned my head away and passed them quickly.

He had to always plan stuff, just in case.

"Can you feel it when you're about to have a seizure?" I asked. My uncle hadn't. His seizures came upon him out of the blue and he'd collapse on the floor, his body convulsing. He'd lived with us, since he hadn't been able to take care of himself, so a seizure was something I was quite familiar with. But I couldn't think about my uncle. Not now, not with the nightmares too fresh in my mind. Not around Geir.

"Most of the time," Geir replied. "Sometimes they spring on me, but usually I have what they call an aura. It can last from minutes to hours, but at least I know a seizure will happen eventually. An aura's a partial seizure, and it's almost always followed by a tonic-clonic seizure." His gaze swivelled over to me for a moment before he looked skywards. "The aura might be different from time to time, too. At times I only feel lightheaded or dizzy, other times I might be flooded with unusual emotions or intense feelings of mental discomfort. It can be a foreboding. I've even experienced hallucinations. Other times vision and hearing might be altered, so I can't hear or see what's around or ahead of me. I've had all those symptoms, several times. Dad says they can be really scary, and some of them can be. Some I don't even remember." He shrugged.

"I guess you had that altered vision and hearing aura when I met you," I told him quietly. "You just stood there, looking ahead. You wouldn't answer me."

Red crept up his cheeks, even more so than what was previously there from the cold. "I'm sorry. I don't remember that. But I guess it's really freaky for those who experience me when I'm having those auras. Dad says so, anyway."

"It *was* freaky." I buried my hands in my pockets to shield them from the cold wind that blew past us. "But I guess that was because I didn't know what it was. When you lost consciousness and fell to the ground, I *did* know, and then I could finally help you. Well, not help you, per se. But I could carry you inside where it was warm after it was over."

His gaze was back on me, drawing me in again. "You said that morning that you used to know someone who had epilepsy. Was it someone close to you?"

"I— No. No one of importance." That was a blatant lie. Kind of. He wasn't important to me, but even now, years later, the simple thought of him could lead to a flashback or an anxiety attack. I didn't want to have either in front of Geir, or out in public in general, so I quickly shut down every single bad memory.

I could tell from the slight frown on his face that he didn't believe me. But he didn't push, and for that I was grateful.

My uncle, and what he'd done to me, was not something I ever talked about. Not even to Tarjei, and Tarjei had been my best friend since pre-school. He'd been there through everything. He *knew* everything. Every single dirty detail. But we never talked about it, and that was the way I wanted it. Because I couldn't talk about it without ending up a complete mess.

"I don't like having epilepsy," he said, shifting the subject back to himself. I was glad. "There are things people take for granted in life that I can't do. Like get my driver's licence—I can't do that. I'm not allowed. I have seizures too often for it to be safe. I have to always be careful. I can't drink alcohol, because that might trigger a seizure, so if I'd *had* any mates, I could never go out for a drink with them. I can't go partying like normal people do."

I bowed my head to stare at the snow-packed ground. "You are different, yes, but you're not abnormal because of it. Don't say that."

If he wasn't normal, what did that make me? I knew very well I wasn't like anyone else. Not anyone

I knew, after all. I had my licence; I had my car and my flat and my education and my work. I had one friend and a big family I'd never been able to get close to.

Well, my closest family I had no desire to be close to, but I had an uncle who was nice and cousins who hadn't done anything wrong. But because my head was messed up, I wasn't as close to them as they were to each other.

I was outside it all.

I wasn't part of anything.

"You're different too." His voice was low, soft.

"What do you mean?" I knew I was different. But he couldn't know why, he couldn't possibly have experienced what I had. *But what if he had?* My blood ran cold at that thought.

"You were kind to me. You helped me out when I had a seizure. You let me in your *bed*. You helped me in school when my classmates were being cruel to me. You're here, now, talking to me like I actually matter. No one else ever does that."

"You do," I insisted. "You do matter. You're a nice lad. The rest of them just can't see that. I don't know why. People can be so cruel at times." I was an expert on that, wasn't I? I knew just how cruel people *could* be. I had severe personal experience in the matter.

He smiled again, stepped closer, and grabbed my

arm. I didn't think he meant to, because when I jerked away, he let go as if he'd been burned.

"I'm sorry. I didn't think. I'm sorry." He held his arms up at chest-level, with his palm out. The universal sign for being unarmed or meaning no harm. "I just— Thank you for saying that. I didn't mean to touch you. I guess I'm just a touchy kind of person when someone is nice to me." He buried his hands in his pockets and hunched his shoulders.

I felt bad for him. He'd just tried to be nice. To show his appreciation for what I'd said. "Don't apologise. It's not your fault I'm—"

I knew the end to that sentence; I just couldn't get it out. *Messed up*. I *was* messed up. I knew that. But I was dealing.

He looked at me with a frown, like he was confused and couldn't figure me out. It was probably the truth, too, because how could he figure me out? Most days I didn't even know what went on in my own head.

"I think you're great."

Just that. Those four words. I turned my head away because I couldn't bear to look at him anymore. How could I be great? I was dealing with so many issues I didn't know where one began and the other ended.

I didn't reply. I didn't know *what* to reply with.

We were reaching the road leading back up to the graveyard now. We'd just have to walk through a path covered on both sides and overhead with trees before we'd reach the gravel roads of the graveyard.

When we did reach the graveyard, I looked around. Gravestones were spread out ahead of us, the lawn separated by the gravel paths. There was one parallel to us, the main road, and several paths crossing from ours to the main one as we walked.

"My mum is buried here," Geir said. "Do you mind if we stop by for a bit?"

I shook my head. "Of course not."

So that answered my question about the mum.

I had people I knew buried in the graveyard too. My uncle, a person I particularly didn't care about, and I carefully avoided looking back in the direction of that gravestone. Kay was out there too, but that was another I couldn't bear to look at.

Geir stopped in front of a neatly tended gravestone. I hovered behind him, still on the road. I wanted to give him his space. He didn't really do anything, just crouched down in front of the big black rock and looked wistfully at the golden writing.

"Dad got a new stone for her last year." Geir glanced up at me briefly. "The old one was weathered, and it wasn't as nice because Dad didn't have much money back when she died. This one, though... this one's perfect." Geir reached out to brush away the few clumps of snow clinging to the stone.

I saw the inscription.

Sunniva Berger.
　　Mum and wife.
　　You will always be remembered with love.

It was a nice stone. It even had a small angel on one side, next to the name, and a picture on the other.

I took a few steps forward to look at it properly. She was blonde with green eyes, exactly like her son. Her smile too was reminiscent of his. She was beautiful. She was young. I looked at the date. It had been a long time since she'd died, when Geir was only seven years old, going by the date.

He'd basically grown up without a mum, a mum who probably had cared for him a great deal. Why did the parents that loved their children die too young, while the parents who hated theirs and ruined their lives got to live?

"How did she die?" I crouched down next to him.

"Cancer. Ovarian cancer." Geir reached out to trace the golden writing again. "They caught it too late. There wasn't much they could do. She died quickly." His shoulders drooped and he swallowed audibly.

I put a hand on his shoulder and squeezed. Funny thing with the whole touching business was that I didn't much mind when *I* was the one doing the touching. I only minded people touching me. But then again, that was a direct result of my childhood, wasn't it?

"I can't really remember her." Geir's fingers brushed over her picture now. "Sometimes I think that the only reason I know what she looks like is because of the pictures Dad kept. I can't remember anything concrete about her."

Wouldn't it be nice not to remember? To not have to relive my childhood at every possible turn.

It would've been nice to forget it all.

To be a normal, functioning human being.

To be able to be touched without instinctively flinching away.

To have a proper relationship with someone.

What would that be like? To be with someone in all senses of the word. To love and to be loved. I had no idea. I'd never experienced love.

"Jørgen?"

I startled out of my thoughts to find his eyes boring into me. "What?" It came out harsher than I'd meant it to, but he'd caught me off guard. For a moment I'd forgotten he was even there as I delved into my own thoughts. I stood up and backed off, back to the gravel road.

"You zoned out on me there." He stood up as well and brushed his hands over his clothes. "You were staring at the stone with a faraway look, like you didn't even see it. Are you okay?"

I nodded jerkily. "Y-yeah. I'm fine."

I wasn't.

I never was.

I was drowning.

Drowning in my own misery.

PART II
I JUST WANT TO BE LOVED

GEIR

CHAPTER 5

*W*hat's wrong with me?

It had to be something, but I couldn't for my life figure out what. Besides the obvious, anyway. My epilepsy. I hated it. I hated living with it, hated how it ruined my life. But besides the epilepsy, I couldn't find anything wrong with me.

Sure, I was small and skinny, but my hair was always washed and well-tended, my skin was smooth, my clothes were nice. I dressed comfortably, usually in loose-fitting jeans, frayed or otherwise, and in tees and jumpers. I wore simple Converse trainers. I was in fashion, such as it was.

I was a nice person, if a bit shy. I was attentive, sensitive, quiet, good at arts. So why didn't anyone like me? I shouldn't have to be alone just because of my epilepsy, but I was. It mattered to everyone. It was a laughing matter when it happened. To them— not to me.

I ran my hand over my face, down my neck, over my collarbone, down my stomach. It wouldn't hurt me to gain a few kilos, but otherwise I was quite content with the way I looked. I couldn't find anything wrong with me. Yet everyone else did.

Tears of frustration rose in my eyes and I angrily wiped them away. I wouldn't cry. I *couldn't* cry. I didn't want to give them that advantage over me. They could tease me, they could be mean to me, but I wouldn't ever cry in front of them.

"Geir?" Dad knocked on my bedroom door before entering.

I quickly turned away from the mirror to face him. I hoped he couldn't see that my eyes were wet. When he only smiled at me, I sighed in relief.

Dad already felt guilty about leaving me alone for so long because of his job. He didn't need to know about my personal problems. There wasn't anything he could do anyway. There wasn't anything *anyone* could do.

"Are you coming down?" Dad nodded towards the now open door. "I tried shouting for you, but you didn't answer. They're here."

"I'm sorry. I was in my own world for a while there." I smiled, hoped it looked genuine.

I followed Dad out of my bedroom and downstairs. When I walked into the living room, I spotted my uncle Daniel, aunt Carina, and my cousin, Marika. They were all smiling at me, and my mood suddenly lifted.

"Happy birthday, Geir!" Marika came forward to hug me. She was four years older than me, but we'd always been close. It had only ever been us, after all. We didn't have any siblings or other cousins. Just the two of us.

My aunt and uncle gave me hugs as well.

"I brought your favourite," aunt Carina said, going over to the coffee table and lifting up a cake container. "Your mum's special chocolate cake."

That sentence made my mouth water.

I loved my mum's chocolate cake. After she'd died, aunt Carina had got my mum's personal cookbook, as neither I nor Dad ever baked. She always made that chocolate cake for me on special occasions.

"Thank you."

She grinned at me and then headed into the kitchen. "Let me get you a piece, love."

Dad's arms wrapped around me. "I know it's not your actual birthday yet, but happy birthday, son. I love you so much."

I turned around so I could hug Dad back. "Thank you. I love you too."

We celebrated my birthday two days early because Dad was leaving for work again tomorrow. I didn't really mind, though it wouldn't be fun spending my birthday alone.

Dad liked his job, and he earned a lot of money doing it. Money that helped pay for the house, the groceries, my medical bills. I always reached the appointed sum for a free card during the year, but it was only February now, and so Dad was the one who had to pay for my medication and medical exams until the sum was reached.

I couldn't begrudge him for wanting to make enough money to make our life comfortable.

"Charlotte's wishing you a happy birthday too." Charlotte was Dad's girlfriend. I'd yet to meet her, though he'd been seeing her for a while. She lived all the way down in Oslo, but they worked together offshore.

I smiled at him, happy she'd do that when she hadn't even met me. "Tell her thanks from me."

"Your gifts are over there. Do you want to open them now?"

I looked over at the coffee table again. My presents were indeed lying there, each wrapped in different paper and just waiting to be opened.

"Yeah." I bit my lip as I walked over. I took the one from Dad first, and he seemed almost more eager than me. I tried to be careful opening the paper, but there was a lot of tape, and I ended up ripping it to pieces. Inside were a brand new sketchbook and a case of my favourite grey drawing pencils, as well as a case of coloured ones. They were the brand I preferred, one of the more expensive ones on the market.

"Thank you, Dad!" It was the perfect gift. I went through sketchbooks and pencils like nothing else.

I reached for the next gift, which was from my uncle and aunt. They'd got me a gift card to the shopping centre, which I would definitely put to use.

"This is wonderful. Thank you!"

I gave Uncle a big smile, as he was the only of the two in the living room.

Marika's gift was last, and I could tell what it was from the shape of it. She'd got me a book on how to draw people. "Amazing! Thank you!" I turned to smile at her. I was good at drawing, but I sometimes had trouble with anatomy. Especially hands. I hated drawing hands. This book would also be put to good use.

Carina came back out into the living room carrying a plate. A big triangle-shaped piece of chocolate cake was on it, and one single candle was put in the middle of it.

"Happy seventeenth!" She handed me the plate and I took it eagerly. I was a bit embarrassed about the candle, but it made them happy, so I played along and blew it out.

Dad handed me an envelope. "I've got this for you too."

I threw him a funny look, but put my plate down and took the envelope from him. Why would he get me two things for my birthday? The sketchbook and pencils had been enough. The pencils themselves weren't exactly cheap. I opened the envelope, ripping it a bit where the glue had taken particularly well.

"Dad!" I looked up from the money inside. "This is too much."

"It's not." He shook his head. "Use that money to take a mate or two to the cinema or go bowling. Do something fun with them."

I could feel my whole face freeze. Take a mate or two to the cinema or to bowling? I didn't *have* a mate, least of all two. But Dad didn't really know that, did he? I'd never told him what a loner I was. He was gone so often that he never questioned the fact that I never had people over. I never brought the subject up either.

"Th-thanks, Dad. I-I will." I held the envelope up and tried for a grin. I could either save the money or add it to the gift card when I went to buy new clothes. My favourite shop wasn't cheap, after all.

Carina had cut up slices of chocolate cake for the others as well, without the birthday light, and we settled down on the sofa, enjoying the sweet cake.

Aunt didn't make it often, only on my birthday and sometimes at Christmas, so I never got tired of it. It was the best part of my birthdays because it was my mum's own recipe, and it kind of felt like she was a part of my special day as well.

DAD LEFT ON SUNDAY AFTERNOON, and I took Charo out for a long walk after I'd hugged him goodbye.

I took the trails up by the graveyard, hoping I would be lucky and meet Jørgen again. I wasn't lucky. He was nowhere to be seen. I took the long route anyway, still enjoying the peace and quiet and the fresh air.

Charo walked calmly next to me. He was too old to run off and play in the snow now, but he was my faithful friend nonetheless. He never strayed far from my side. He was a good dog. The best. He was fiercely loyal to me and to a certain extent, Dad, and he tolerated Uncle, Aunt, and Marika.

That he'd taken so quickly to Jørgen that day had been a surprise, but a very welcome one. If Charo liked Jørgen, there was absolutely no reason for me not to. Jørgen had been so kind to me from our first meeting, the one I couldn't even remember.

Jørgen wasn't just nice, he was handsome too. Very handsome, in fact, with his white-blond hair and pale blue eyes. He was taller than me and wider, but then that didn't take much. Jørgen was slim, though, and, from what I'd seen of him, toned. A perfect, drool-worthy body.

He seemed skittish, especially whenever I'd tried to touch him. He'd said it didn't have anything to do with me and I did believe him, because he'd seemed rather hesitant about touching Charo at first too.

He'd taken to Charo, however, and I couldn't forget the squeeze he'd given my shoulder when I'd crouched in front of my mum's grave. He'd willingly touched me then.

It was just when I touched him he flinched away. I didn't know why, but I could surmise it wasn't anything good. Still, Jørgen was the only one outside my family who was nice to me, and I was smitten. I couldn't stop thinking about him.

I wished I could see him again, but short of

showing up on his doorstep I didn't know how that would happen.

The last time had been a coincidence. We'd both just happened to be on the same place at the same time. I wasn't dumb enough to believe such a coincidence would happen again soon, not even in a small town the size of ours.

When I got home, I gave Charo new water and filled his food bowl, and then I changed into jogging bottoms and a tee.

I curled on the sofa with a bowl of butter-flavoured popcorn and an episode of *Doctor Who* on Netflix.

Charo curled up on the floor beneath me when he'd finished drinking and eating, and the sound of his breathing was a comfort to listen to.

I didn't worry about being home alone as long as I had Charo.

I WOKE up on Monday morning feeling rested.

I was seventeen now.

Not that I felt any different, but being a year older was always good. Only a year until I was eighteen, then only a couple of months after that I would be finished with school.

I could finish after this year, find an apprentice-ship and start working, but I honestly didn't know what to do. So I'd opted to take another year, a year of general studies so that I could choose to go to university if I ever did figure out what I wanted to do with my life.

I ate breakfast, took my medication with the meal, took Charo out so he could relieve himself, and then it was time to go to school.

Mondays were always nice because we started later than any other day of the week. Fridays were nice too, because then we quit earlier than any other day. They organised it that way so that the students that didn't live in town could come back on Monday morning and leave early to go back home for the weekend.

I appreciated it, even if I did live in town and it didn't really affect me. Still, I got to sleep longer on Mondays and got a longer weekend. Win, win.

But school in itself was something I dreaded. I liked my classes all right; it was the rest of my class-mates I had a problem with. Or more correctly, they had a problem with me.

I still hadn't found an answer to my scrutiny on Saturday, but today was my birthday, so I resolved to not let them ruin it. Not that my birthday would be any special, as Dad had left, but it was still my birthday. It was special to *me*.

Of course, when I'd decided not to let them ruin my day, they did exactly that. The one who always started it, Jonas, was the one everyone in class gathered around. The one every girl fancied. He, especially, seemed to have it in for me, and everyone else followed his lead.

As I had headed to the corner desk in the back of the classroom, the one where I could hide and no one would really bother me, Jonas stuck his foot out to trip me. I lost my balance and fell painfully to the floor.

My rucksack, which had only been hanging on one shoulder, slid to the floor, and a couple of schoolbooks as well as my sketchbook slid out. I'd opened it outside to put my sketchbook back before going into the classroom, and I hadn't thought about closing it.

I regretted that now as Jonas shot off his chair and grabbed my sketchbook.

My wrists hurt from taking the fall of my entire body, but I didn't want Jonas to look in that book. So I pushed up, even if it was painful, and I made to grab it back. "Give it back."

"What have you got hidden in here?" Jonas danced

out of my way and he flipped the book open. He rifled through the pages until he came to the last one. The one I definitely didn't want him to see. The one where I'd sketched Jørgen's downturned profile. The page where I'd thoughtlessly written Jørgen's name inside a heart.

"Is this your boyfriend?" Jonas taunted, turning the page around so I and everyone else in the classroom could see it. My face flamed red. "Of course you're a poof," Jonas continued, "that much has always been obvious. You're a right little nancyboy."

"Give it back." My voice shook. It wouldn't endear me in any of their eyes; it would only serve to prove Jonas' statement. I couldn't help it, though. I was upset and it wasn't something I could hide easily. "Please. Give it back."

Jonas snorted and threw the sketchbook at my chest.

I didn't react quickly enough to catch it, and it fell to the floor in a flurry of pages. I quickly scooped down to retrieve it. Some of the pages were bent, but I smoothed them out as well as I was able to. Then I gathered up my pack and the other books that had slid out.

I cast Jonas a nervous look as I stood up again, but he'd turned away from me. A couple of my classmates were snickering, and I bowed my head as I shuffled to the back of the classroom.

I knew my face was still red, and my eyes burned with unshed tears.

Why did they have to be so cruel?

What had I ever done to them to deserve such treatment?

CHAPTER 6

*A*ll in all, it was one of my worst days at school.

Now that Jonas had new ammunition to use against me, he went out of his way to make recess as miserable as possible for me.

There wasn't anything fun about the day at all.

I couldn't concentrate on classes.

I couldn't even concentrate on my sketching, not after Jonas had seen what I drew.

I didn't know what I wanted to draw if I couldn't draw Jørgen, and I didn't dare draw him in school in case someone saw and started teasing me even more.

So I sat with my mobile, looking through the cinema program for the evening. Dad had given me money to take a mate or two out. I didn't have one, but that didn't mean I couldn't go to the cinema by myself.

Or... maybe there was someone I could ask? Someone who'd only been nice to me since we met. Someone I desperately wanted to see again, but didn't know how to go about it.

Maybe this was the perfect excuse.

I could always ask Marika, but then she'd know what a complete loser I was.

Jørgen, on the other hand... Aside from the whole touching thing, he didn't really seem to mind being around me. I could, maybe, go as far as to say he liked me.

By the time classes were done, I'd made up my mind.

I didn't know how long Jørgen was at work, so I went home after school. I threw my rucksack away the moment I stepped through the door, startling Charo, who'd come trotting out from the living room to greet me.

"Hey, boy." I bent down to pet him and ended up burying my face in his soft fur. "Why is everything so hard? Why don't they like me?"

Charo didn't have an answer for me. He simply turned his head so he could lick my face.

"Come on, boy, let's go for a walk." I snapped the leash on him and we headed outside. I always had a leash when we were out in residential areas, but whenever we went to the trails around the graveyard or anywhere else where there was only nature, I always let him loose.

I didn't go to the graveyard. I went towards the school for general studies instead.

There was a big outdoor area spanning out from behind the school. There were a couple of trails, but mostly it was outcrops and grassland. We were close to the sea, and though the sea itself wasn't frozen, there was a bit of ice on the shallower grounds closest to shore. Charo went down to sniff the thin ice, but he didn't touch it.

It was nice being outside with just Charo for company. Charo liked me no matter what. He'd never talk down to me or be cruel for the simple pleasure of seeing me upset. The only thing Charo did was rub up against me and lick my hand in affection.

When we got home, the clock was nearing five.

We'd been out a while and I was freezing.

After making myself a big cup of hot chocolate, I curled up under my blanket on the sofa.

I was just going to get some warmth back into me, and then I was going to head over to Jørgen's place. The film didn't start for a couple of hours, so I had a lot of time. I was afraid that if I didn't simply man up and do it now, I wouldn't do it at all. Better get it over with.

I drained the hot chocolate once it'd cooled off a bit, then changed out Charo's water and filled his food bowl.

"You be nice while I'm gone."

I crouched down to give him a proper goodbye, complete with him licking my face and me hugging him tight between the petting. It wasn't like I had to tell him to be a good boy, because he always was. He never barked when he was alone, at least not as far as I knew.

The neighbours had never complained, in any case.

Dressing in my outerwear again, I headed outside.

It had started to snow lightly while I'd been inside. Tiny white snowflakes drifted slowly down to ground in the darkening evening. It was beautiful. The thing I loved most about Norway was the seasons. All four were so distinct, and all had their own beauty to them. Winter, when all was covered in white. Spring, when the snow had melted and everything started to bloom again. Summer, with the vibrant colours and nicer weather. Then autumn, when the colours of summer turned even more colourful and darker, before giving way to winter.

The lights from Jørgen's living room windows could be seen from the street, even if they were curtained.

My stomach started doing cartwheels as I stood there, looking up. Jørgen was in there, and if I could dredge up the courage I'd finally see him again. I hadn't been able to stop thinking about him. He'd been on my mind constantly ever since the first time I met him.

I knew I was smitten, but I couldn't help it. He was gorgeous, he was nice, and he actually gave me the time of day.

I strode up to the door and rang the bell before I could let my nerves get the better of me. I buried my hands in my jacket pockets because I'd forgotten to bring gloves when I'd left home—I'd been too nervous to even think about it.

The door opened and Jørgen stood there, illuminated by the light inside the flat. I looked up at him, completely mesmerised by the sight of him. I couldn't tell what he thought about seeing me, because he was always so expressionless.

"Hi." The words came out no louder than a whisper. I cleared my throat.

"Hi." Jørgen's pale blue gaze locked on me, and I swallowed nervously.

How could I possibly get anything coherent out

when he stared at me? He made me weak in the knees by just being in my vicinity, and having his complete focus on *me* caused my stomach to start doing cartwheels.

"I was wondering…" I didn't know how to phrase my question. I hadn't really thought that far. I wish I had. "Wouldyouliketogotothecinemawithme?"

Jørgen continued to stare at me for a moment. I could see his jaw clenching, and my chest tightened painfully. Suddenly, emotions welled up and I fought tears again, just like earlier in school.

"Please don't say no." I wasn't above begging. I really wasn't. "Please, Jørgen. I just want a friend." I wouldn't touch him; I wouldn't do anything to make him back away from me, not if he wanted me around. All I wanted was a friend. I'd give anything to have just *one* friend. If Jørgen couldn't be anything else, I hoped he at least could be that.

His expression softened and he moved out of the way.

I took that to be an invitation and stepped inside. I stopped right inside the doorway, not wanting to go further in with snow clinging to my boots.

He closed the door behind me, leaning close to me to do so.

"Which film do you want to see?" He was at a respectable distance again now that he'd closed the door. I wouldn't mind if he stood closer, but if he only wanted to be friends, then I would respect that.

"The new *Varg Veum*?" I didn't know why that came out as a question. That was the film I wanted to go see, but maybe he didn't want to see it. Maybe Norwegian crime films weren't his cup of tea. I wasn't much for crime dramas either, but I actually did enjoy that particular series.

"When does it start?" Jørgen twined his fingers together like I did sometimes when I was nervous. Was he nervous about something? About being around me? About going to the cinema?

"At nine. So it's a while, still." Did that mean he wanted to go with me? I hoped he did. I really wanted to see the film before it stopped showing, but I didn't want to go alone. I wanted to go with Jørgen. If he said no, I would just go back home and watch something on Netflix.

"Okay." He nodded. "Want to come in, then?" He motioned towards the living room.

The thing about Jørgen's flat was that it was very open. The hallway was the most closed off part of it. The living room was big and the kitchen had an open plan. The bedroom had a sliding door, but the last time I was there it was open, and it was now too. The bathroom had a proper door, also wide open. Jørgen seemed a fan of open spaces.

I bent to undo the laces on my boots, and then I put them away and hung my jacket up.

Jørgen walked over to the sofa, where he sat down directly facing the telly. I sat down a good distance from him, curled my legs under me, and rested my hands in my lap. Now that I was there, I didn't know what to say, and the silence felt strained and awkward.

"Happy birthday," he said suddenly, bringing my head up.

He looked back at me.

"Th-thanks." I stared at him in surprise. "How'd you know it's my birthday?"

"When you had your seizure, I went through your bag to see if I could find someone to contact. I found your ID, but that was it. I remember the date. It's easy to remember, after all, with it being Valentine's Day."

I blushed. I didn't have a problem with him going through my bag. I would've done the same too if a strange kid had passed out in my bed. That he pointed out today was Valentine's, however, that got me. Valentine's Day wasn't such a big deal, but still... it meant *something*.

"Yeah. Seventeen. Doesn't feel much different from being sixteen, really." There was nothing good about being seventeen. Had I been eighteen, I could've bought beer or smokes—not that I needed any of them, but I could've bought it if I'd felt like it. I could've got a proper debit card, which I could use to shop online. I could've got my licence, if I'd been allowed to. Eighteen was special. Seventeen, not so much.

"Have you had a nice day?"

I tensed up at that, not knowing what to say.

"Not really, no." I settled for being honest. If I wanted him to be my friend, I should definitely be honest with him.

I wanted him to be honest with me too.

"We celebrated my birthday on Saturday because Dad had to leave for work again on Sunday. My aunt made my mum's special chocolate cake. I got a new sketchbook, pencils, a drawing reference book, and a gift card to the shopping centre. That was nice. Today... not so much." I shrugged awkwardly. "There's this bloke—Well, you met him. Jonas. He goes out of his way to make life miserable for me. Today was especially bad."

Jørgen looked at me, sort of contemplative. "What did he do?"

I grimaced. "What he always does. He trips me. Shoves me. Taunts me. Calls me names. It's not really anything I'm not used to, but as today is my birthday,

I guess it feels even worse than usual. I did want to, for once, have a nice day."

"Kids can be cruel."

"I'm not really a kid." Was that the way he looked at me? As a kid? I was seventeen years old. I might not have been legal for much, but I *was* legal for sex. Had been for a year.

It was a bit ridiculous that you could have sex and children legally at sixteen, but you weren't legal in any other sense until you were eighteen. But that was Norway for you, wasn't it? It didn't make sense.

He smiled slightly at me then, and my breath hitched. He was beautiful when he smiled. "Teenagers, then. Teenagers can be cruel."

I had first-hand experience. I knew it all too well, and I hated it.

"Why do you think they singled me out?" My voice was small now. It wasn't something I particularly wanted to talk about, but who else could I actually talk to? There was only Jørgen. "Do you think it's only because of my epilepsy?"

"I don't know." Jørgen finally averted his eyes, and I wasn't sure if I was relieved or disappointed. Maybe a mix of both. "Might be for you. For me, I guess..." He got a faraway look on his face, then he shook his head. "I don't know what it was for me."

I sat up straighter. "Were people cruel to you as

well, when you were in school?" It wasn't that I wanted it to be so, but if it was... Well, we'd have something in common then, wouldn't we? All I wanted was something in common with him. Even this.

"No, not my classmates. It was more that they didn't give me the time of day. Like I didn't exist. I didn't want to draw any attention to myself either, but it was lonely. I mean, I had my friend Tarjei, but he's a totally different person from me. It got lonely sometimes, I guess, but at the same time I preferred it." The faraway look was back.

I didn't like it.

He shook his head again, as if he needed to clear his thoughts. He probably did.

His words resonated in my mind. He hadn't gone through the same as I did, but he'd been an outsider too. *Not my classmates.*

A thought struck me. Had someone else been cruel to him? I doubted he'd want to talk about it, considering how he'd skirted away from anything personal back at the cemetery or when we'd been sitting on the bench. I decided to let the subject drop. I didn't want to alienate him by bringing up something potentially traumatic.

"Jonas found out I was gay today," I said. I hoped he wouldn't turn out to be a homophobic person. He seemed okay with my epilepsy—where everyone else minded it—so maybe he would be okay with this too? "That gave him even more ammunition to use against me."

Jørgen leaned back to rest his head on the back of the sofa. "Maybe he fancies you."

I couldn't help the laugh that slipped out at that. "You're mental. Jonas? Fancy me? No way."

Jørgen turned to me. "A lot of the time, it's the ones that taunt loudest that have something to hide."

I shook my head. "I don't—You really think so?" It couldn't be. He had to be mistaken, but now that the words were out there... maybe there was something to them.

"Maybe he's afraid of his own sexuality, and so he takes it out on you. That's usually why people bully. Because they don't particularly like themselves. Of course, some are just arseholes, there will always be a percentage of those, but otherwise..." He shrugged. "It's not impossible."

"I guess not." I was still doubtful, but the thought was somewhat uplifting.

Maybe there wasn't anything particularly wrong with me; maybe the problem lay with Jonas himself.

I much preferred that way of thinking about it.

I smiled at Jørgen. "I never would've thought to put it that way."

He turned his head away again, but I could see that the corner of his lip tilted up slightly.

I liked to see him smile.

I hadn't seen it much, but when I actually did, it was nice.

He should smile often.

CHAPTER 7

*T*here weren't many people at the cinema.

The film was being shown in the small theatre, and there were only a few others there besides us. We had the entire back row to ourselves, which was quite nice. What I didn't like about the cinema was sitting squished between people. Especially not strangers.

Jørgen was tense beside me and he had his hands crossed over his chest.

He avoided putting his arm close to my seat—he even avoided the armrest, which I supposed was meant for both of us.

He'd argued about paying for the tickets, but I'd told him that Dad had given me money especially for this purpose and he'd eventually relented. He'd let me pay. I was quite happy about that fact.

He'd only bought water for himself, where I'd bought a Cola and a snack-box that was split in two, one half with salted popcorn and the other with bacon crisps.

We'd arrived early, but we sat in silence while we waited for the lights to dim and for the commercials to start. The fifteen minutes of commercials were the most boring part about going to the cinema, but it was usually well worth it once the film started.

When it did, I held my box out to Jørgen. "Want to taste?"

He glanced at me, then down at the snacks. "No, thanks."

"I'm putting it here in case you change your mind. Just take some. I don't mind." I smiled at him as I wedged the rectangle box between my thigh and the armrest. He didn't reply to that, but that was okay. Jørgen never said much unless he was prompted, as I'd figured out in the past few hours.

What he did say was usually worth listening to though.

The film started with a *bam* as Varg Veum witnessed a young girl being murdered in front of him.

That was what I always liked about these films:

something happened at every turn, and Varg Veum was always smack in the middle of it. It didn't hurt that the actor who played Varg Veum was rather handsome. He didn't have anything on Jørgen, of course, but he was easy on the eyes and made the film even more enjoyable.

Halfway through, I lifted the box up again. "Sure you don't want a taste?" I whispered, shaking it a little. I'd eaten my fair share of both sides.

Jørgen hesitated, but he did eventually reach out to take one bacon crisp. It was better than nothing, so I put the box back between my thigh and the armrest. I doubted he'd reach over to take something, but I continued to prod through the movie, and he ate a couple more bacon crisps before he told me no again.

When he wasn't eating or drinking from his water bottle, he had his arms firmly crossed over his chest. He still seemed tense, though a bit less than before the film had started.

When the film ended, with Varg Veum solving the mystery and not really being appreciated much for it, Jørgen stretched as he stood. I couldn't help but stare. He reached back to grab his jacket, which he'd discarded on the chair on his other side.

I mimicked him in pulling my own jacket on.

"Did you like it?" I asked as we emerged back out on the street.

"Yeah. It was okay." He buried his hands in his jacket pockets as he smiled slightly at me. His gaze roamed our surroundings. "Are you hungry?"

"Uh." I hadn't eaten anything since lunch, had I? I'd only had that cup of hot chocolate after I'd walked Charo. "Yeah, I guess."

"Care for fast food?" Jørgen nodded towards one of the town's many fast food shops across the street. "They've got decent food there."

"Okay." I had fast food once in a while, when Dad wasn't home, or when I wasn't over at Aunt and Uncle's for dinner, or when I couldn't be bothered to make something myself.

I'd never actually tried that shop before, though.

Jørgen held the door open for me so I could go in before him. I looked up at the big board above the counter to see what they had to choose from. They had the usual: pizzas, burgers, kebabs, chicken, beef.

"Do you want one of the dinners or should we split a pizza?" Jørgen came up on my side.

Splitting a pizza definitely meant spending more time with him. I didn't think he'd leave me to eat alone if I chose something else either, but still. And I actually did want pizza.

"Pepperoni pizza?" That was my favourite. A bit spicy, but not too much.

Jørgen nodded, then promptly stepped up to the

counter to order. The man behind the counter spoke only broken Norwegian, but Jørgen managed to get his point across anyway.

When the cashier asked if we wanted to eat there or bring it with us, Jørgen said we'd take it to go.

My stomach leapt.

That meant spending more time with Jørgen in his flat. Or maybe we would go our separate ways.

My stomach plummeted.

Jørgen turned to me. "Want a sauce?"

I thought quickly. Garlic or... "Sour cream?"

Jørgen nodded and turned back around to deliver the information. The bloke behind the bar told us it'd take ten to fifteen minutes, so Jørgen and I ventured back outside. It was better than sitting inside waiting.

It was bloody cold out, though, and I rubbed my hands together. I still didn't have my gloves.

"We can go back in if you're cold." Jørgen looked pointedly at my hands.

"That's okay. It's too stifling inside. I'd much rather stay here." It was true. Being wrapped up in winter gear didn't make for comfort wherever it was actually warm. My jacket was thick, made for the cold winters we had, and I wore long underwear underneath my jeans as well as thick, furred boots and wool socks. It was only my hands that were the problem. I should start keeping my gloves in my pockets so I'd stop forgetting them.

Jørgen glanced around. It was almost like he didn't want his eyes to settle on me. "Do you have school tomorrow?"

"Yeah."

I didn't want to, but I missed enough school whenever I had a seizure. If I had one during the school day or the morning, I'd have to sleep after and then I tended to miss a lot.

So when I didn't have a seizure, I'd go to school no matter what. I wanted to graduate with the best possible grades I could get. I wouldn't earn them by skipping. I had to endure. Even if dread settled heavy in my stomach at the thought.

"Hey." Jørgen's voice was gentle.

He took a gentle grip on my chin and tilted my head up. I wasn't even aware I'd bowed it, honestly. And there he was, reaching out to me because of it. His hand shook slightly, but I didn't mind as long as he kept on touching me. I looked into his eyes and there was something there... but I didn't know him enough to figure out exactly what it was. "If he says anything to you, or does anything, just think about the big gay crush he actually has on you."

I laughed.

I couldn't help it.

The mere thought of it was too funny.

"There." Jørgen's thumb flicked briefly over my lower lip, but he retracted his hand before I could really believe it had happened. Still, my lip tingled, and it was definitely not from the cold. "I like it much better when you smile."

I was lost for words.

Jørgen had admitted to liking my smile.

My stomach did cartwheels again now, and it was wonderful.

He seemed to have spoken without meaning to, as a faint blush coloured what I could see of his neck as well as the sides of his cheeks. He turned his head away from me, presumably to stop me from seeing it, but I still did.

I couldn't stop looking at him.

I'd notice anything, no matter what small a change it might be.

We stood in silence.

I didn't think either of us knew what to say after Jørgen's words. He seemed to feel awkward, while I felt rather light and happy.

He *liked* me. Well, he'd said he liked me better when I smiled, but it amounted to the same thing, didn't it? Jørgen liked *me*. And he'd actually touched me, skin on skin and all, even if was just his fingers grabbing my chin.

He stepped around me suddenly, startling me out of my thoughts. He once again held the door open for me and I went inside, quickly followed by him.

The bloke behind the counter was wrapping up our pizza box in a bag.

Jørgen went up to the counter and paid, then took the bag. I followed him back outside again without a word. Jørgen had driven us down to the cinema, so we got back into his car and headed back to his flat.

I felt relaxed now, even if we still hadn't talked after what he'd said.

I didn't mind.

The butterflies were dancing in my stomach, and I finally felt *good*. He made me feel good. It was a nice feeling, one I was unfamiliar with. When did I ever really feel good? School didn't make me feel good about myself, and when I came home I was upset about whatever had happened during the day. The only time I could relax was in the weekends, but then I usually spent them dreading going back to school Monday.

"Are you okay?" Jørgen looked over at me as he parked his car outside his flat.

"Yeah." I smiled. "I'm good."

His face was expressionless as he studied me. He didn't question me though, instead he got out, got the pizza from the backseat, and headed towards the front door.

I was right behind him, shuddering a bit in the cold, dark night.

It was late.

It must be close to eleven by now.

I had school in the morning, Jørgen probably had work, but I couldn't bring myself to go home.

I wanted to spend every second I could with him.

Jørgen put the pizza box on the coffee table, then he disappeared into the kitchen, returning with two plates, cutlery, and napkins.

I opened the pizza box, folding the upper part of it under so it wouldn't take too much space on the table.

We settled down comfortably to eat. The pizza was warm, and with a dash of sour cream spread out on top, it tasted like heaven. Store-bought pizza never held anything to take-out pizza. But then, take-out pizza never held anything to homemade pizza. Especially not my dad's.

"Do you cook much?" I asked, curious. Jørgen had a big, modern kitchen. I reckoned it would be a joy to work in.

"Not really, no." Jørgen shrugged. "Just easy stuff. I'm not much of a cook, really."

"I like to cook, if I've got the time for it and everything I need around me." I had to like cooking if I wanted to survive on my own. I didn't mind it at all. It was fun to make food, especially when I made dinner for me and Dad. It wasn't as much fun cooking only for myself though.

"I guess we're quite different. I don't really have the patience for proper cooking." He grinned slightly before taking another bite of his pizza slice.

"Maybe I should cook for you, then," I dared to suggest.

His grin faded as his gaze snapped to me. I couldn't tell what he thought about my suggestion, but I prayed silently it wasn't anything bad. That he wouldn't push me away.

"Maybe you could. Sometime."

That was a lot better than I'd hoped for. He wanted to spend time with me beyond today.

"I will." Most definitely. I wasn't an excellent cook, I knew that, but I could whip together a lot of different meals.

We settled back into silence as we ate more of the pizza.

When I finished and checked my mobile, I saw that it was already eleven-thirty. I'd gone from such a shitty day to having a pretty good evening, and I didn't want it to end.

But I needed my sleep. Proper sleep, proper

meals, and taking my medication at the same time every day kept my seizures at bay longer and tended to keep them lighter.

"I have to go home." I cast Jørgen a regretful look. "I've got school and I'm guessing you've got work." I carried both my own and his plate into the kitchen, rinsing and washing them in the sink, then put them away to dry.

"I've got a dishwasher," Jørgen said from the doorway.

"I know, but it's only two plates and some cutlery. No reason to put them in the washer when it's easier to simply wash them."

Jørgen walked back over to the coffee table, where he shut the pizza box. We still had some left. "You want to take this with you?"

I shook my head. "It's your pizza. You paid for it. You can have it for breakfast tomorrow."

"So could you." He put the box down on the kitchen counter.

"How about we split the rest of it?" I compromised.

Jørgen nodded and pulled a plastic box down from inside one of the cabinets. Almost half the pizza was left, and he took half of the remaining pieces and put them in the plastic box. He handed it to me, and my skin tingled as our fingers brushed. He didn't jerk away this time, so maybe the touch had been expected.

"I'll drive you home."

"Oh, no, you don't have to do that. It's not far. I'll walk." It was late. I didn't want to take more of his time, even if I did want to be around him even longer. He needed his sleep too.

"Can I hug you?" I bit my lip.

I hadn't meant to ask that, it had just come out without any kind of censoring from my brain. He'd been so kind to me, kinder than anyone else ever was, except my family. And he seemed so jumpy around people, but he was here with me, and I just...

I just wanted a hug.

CHAPTER 8

*H*e looked taken aback and blinked down at me. "Uh. Yeah. I guess."

I put the box I'd been clutching on the counter and stepped up to him.

He stood stock-still, not moving, and I slid my arms tentatively around his torso. I made the hug light—I didn't want it to seem like I clung to him—and his stiff body told me loud and clear he wasn't comfortable. It was a shame, because hugging him did feel rather good.

"Thank you," I whispered, meaning it with all my heart. "Thank you for being kind to me. For not pushing me away today. I meant what I said, I just want a friend, and you've been so wonderful to me."

His arms hesitantly came up to settle on my back,

hugging me in return, even if it was done rather awkwardly. He didn't say anything, but he didn't need to. I knew he didn't like to be touched, at least not if it came on unexpectedly, but this was very expected. Very nice.

He felt good against me, all hard, warm body. He smelled faintly of cologne, and I was struck by a sudden desire to run my lips down his throat.

I knew he wouldn't appreciate it, so I didn't do it, but the desire was there and it was *strong*.

"I'll drive you home, Geir." Jørgen said it with a finality I didn't want to challenge, not when his arms were around me and I was pressed up against him. "That way you'll get home quicker and I won't have to worry."

"You'd worry about me?" I mumbled against the fabric of his jumper. "What's there to worry about?"

"This might be a small town, but a lot can happen even here." One of his hands inched up my back to settle over my left shoulder blade. The other stayed on my lower back.

I took notice of him completely ignoring my first question, but that was answer enough in itself. He would worry about me, exactly like he'd said. He'd *worry*.

It made me feel all warm and tingly, and I wanted to cling to him and never let him go. He felt good pressed up against me. Our bodies fit together nicely, like we were made for each other.

It was cliché, I knew, but I wanted something cliché. I didn't want to be the freak with the seizures, the one everyone made fun off. I wanted someone to love me for who I was—I wanted someone to simply want to be with *me*. Was that too much to ask for?

Jørgen eventually pulled back. His face was flushed. I liked that the blush crept up his neck, whereas on me it went straight for the cheeks. It was subtler, but at the same time quite obvious.

"Thank you," I whispered again. I didn't know why. I'd already said my piece, but it slipped out again anyway.

He looked at me, his pale eyes unreadable. Then he motioned towards the hall. "Come on. You need your sleep."

I wasn't quite sure how to take that, but I did follow him out of the kitchen after grabbing my plastic box. Did he mean I needed my sleep because I was young? Or... He'd seemed to know about epilepsy before, so maybe he knew how important a proper sleeping pattern was? If so, it was actually kind of nice.

I bundled up in my clothes, and before I knew it, we were in his car and he pulled away from the kerb.

It only took about five minutes to my home, and the trip was over before I even knew it.

The house was dark and uninviting. Charo was probably asleep and waiting for me.

I reached for the door handle, then stopped and turned to him.

"Can I get your number?"

I wanted to be able to contact him. I hoped he wouldn't mind. I fumbled my mobile out of my pocket and held it out to him.

He stared at it a moment, but took it from me. He programmed his number into my contacts list and promptly handed it back.

"Do you want mine?" I asked.

His gaze met mine, as unreadable as ever. He handed me his phone, and I was pleasantly surprised to see it was the same one I had. I programmed my own name into his contacts list, first and last name both, then handed it back with a smile.

"Thanks for tonight." I groped for the handle and got out of the car. I bent back down to get a good look at him one last time. There was a street light right above the windshield, so I could see him clearly even if it was pitch black outside. "I hope it won't be long until next time."

He was silent again for a few moments, but then he smiled. It was just an upturn of one corner of his mouth, but I'd seen it enough now to know it equaled a smile for him. "Goodnight, Geir. Sleep well."

"You too." I turned and hurried up the steps.

I unlocked the front door, and when I pulled it open, I heard him drive away. I turned to watch the taillights disappear down the street. When he was out of sight, I stepped inside, turned on the light in the hallway, and locked the door safely after me.

Charo came into the hallway. He stretched and yawned halfway to me.

"Hey, boy. Have you been a good while I've been gone?" I reached down to rub him when he reached me, and I got a lick on the cheek in return. "I've had the most wonderful night. My birthday turned out all right after all. Who would've thought, huh?"

Charo followed me upstairs and waited patiently as I got ready for bed.

When I'd finished, I flopped over on my bed, where I fiddled with my mobile. Jørgen had touched it only a little while before. He'd put his number into it.

I had Jørgen's mobile number.

It was exhilarating.

I wanted to send him a message right away, just to make sure it really was his number. Not that I believed he'd give me the wrong one, but still... it was a bit hard to believe that I finally had it after a month of thinking about him constantly.

It would be desperate to send him a text now, wouldn't it? We'd just parted ways.

But I really wanted to see him again, and I didn't want to wait.

I didn't know what to ask him, though. There wasn't much to do in town, and even if there were, I didn't do any of it. The only things I did were walk Charo and curl up with Netflix at the end of the day. There was homework somewhere in there too.

I unlocked my screen and clicked in on his name in my contacts.

Jørgen Lister.

So that was his full name. My thumb hovered over *send a message*, but I finally clicked it.

A new, empty conversation opened.

I let my fingers hover over the touch screen, writing in my question before I could change my mind.

Do you want to walk Charo with me tomorrow?

The moment the message was sent, I started doubting myself.

Why had I sent him a message so quickly after parting from him? I'd seem desperate, pathetic, clingy... I didn't want to seem like any of those things, but at the same time I didn't want to wait.

Impatient was a kinder word, I supposed, but was that what he would think when he saw that message? He'd be more likely to use one of the former ones.

I almost dropped my mobile in shock when it pinged.

I couldn't see who it was from as I hadn't locked my screen. There was only a bright red circle showing the number one over the message symbol.

I clicked it, my heart beating twice as much as it usually did.

Jørgen: Yeah, sure.

It wasn't the longest answer, or the most enthusiastic one, but he'd said *yes*!

I couldn't have asked for more than that.

Jørgen had said yes to seeing me tomorrow, no matter what he thought about me texting him so quickly after our parting tonight.

Maybe he didn't think any of those things I'd just thought about myself.

Maybe he was just lonely too and needed a friend?

~

I DIDN'T KNOW if it was my exceptionally good mood or not, but the next day seemed a lot easier to deal with than the previous one.

Jonas didn't try to trip me, even though he did shove me into the wall once at break. He did rattle off some homophobic bullocks, but I was too busy thinking about what would happen after school to pay him much attention.

I wasn't dumb enough to think it would continue to be like that.

Jonas' slurs would probably bother me more tomorrow, but for now my mind was too busy with Jørgen saying yes to spending time with me to be able to focus on anything else.

I couldn't help opening my sketchbook throughout the day to sketch him, though I refrained from writing his name just in case Jonas got a hold of it again.

The day dragged, but the last class finally ended and everyone started packing their books.

For once I was out the door before many of the others. I usually tended to wait to be last, but not today.

Today I had something to look forward to.

I knew Jørgen wouldn't be off work yet; it was too

early for that. If he worked regular hours it would be at least another hour and a half, but I was excited and I couldn't help it.

Someone bumped into me, hard, almost sending me sprawling to the ground.

I managed to keep my balance, but I clutched my shoulder strap tighter as I looked to my side.

Jonas leered at me.

"I'm sorry," he said. "I didn't see you there." With that, he sauntered off with his mates, laughing.

Yeah, I just bet he hadn't seen me.

Charo greeted me as usual when I got home. His tail wagged happily as he looked up at me. I bent down to ruffle his fur, then pressed my cheek to the top of his head.

I went into the kitchen to change his water and fill his food bowl, as I did every day. I mixed some liver paste from the fridge with his dry food today.

He deserved it for being such a good, faithful dog. His tail wagged while I mixed it in. If I didn't mix it, he'd just eat the liver paste and leave the kibble.

He was over the bowl the minute I put it on the floor. I watched him with a smile before I went over to the fridge to put the liver paste back and check if there was anything for me to eat.

Dad had stocked it nicely before he left for work, like he always did.

There was a box of chicken filets in there that Dad hadn't put in the freezer. I'd have to eat those before they turned bad.

I chewed on my lower lip, thinking, as I glanced at the clock. Jørgen would still be at work, but he'd promised to walk Charo with me. Would he do it right after work or would he go home to eat first?

He'd admitted he wasn't much of a cook.

I liked to cook.

I had a fully stocked fridge.

It all added up.

I fished my mobile out of my pocket and quickly typed in a message.

If you want to come over right after work, I'll make us both dinner.

It was an awkward message, but I didn't quite know how else to phrase it. It wasn't a question, but it seemed like he didn't have to come if he didn't want to. He certainly had a choice.

Was it phrased so that it sounded like this was something I actually did want to do, though? I wasn't quite sure, but I had no idea what else to write. So I simply added a smiley on the end of the sentence and clicked send before I could change my mind.

After shutting the fridge, I wandered out into the living room while I waited for an answer.

I was nervous anticipating his reply.

I fiddled with my mobile, hoping to hear the tell-tale click of a new message soon so the butterflies didn't have to go wild in my stomach. I needed dinner, he needed sustenance, and I was offering to cook. How could he say no, especially as he'd told me just the night before that he wasn't very keen on cooking?

I went back into the kitchen to check the cupboards. There were all kinds of sauces to choose from as well as pasta and rice. Dad never left without stocking up, so that I wouldn't have to go to the store to do the big purchases. He didn't like me to carry heavy bags. Not that heavy lifting had ever triggered a seizure, but Dad always worried about me. Even more so when he wasn't at home to keep an eye on me.

My mobile vibrated and I almost jumped half a foot in the air. It almost slipped from my fingers, but I managed to hold on to it and fumble it around so I could see the display.

I unlocked it and clicked in on the messages.

He'd answered me.

Jørgen: I'll be over when I'm done at three-thirty.

Another short message from him. I was beginning to suspect he wasn't much of a texter.

I didn't mind at all, because he was coming over.

I stared at the text message for a couple more seconds, and then got moving. I went to the fridge to pull out chicken, onion, lettuce, and cucumber. If we were having chicken filets, we needed a salad. I needed milk too, for the chicken sauce.

Should I make chips or rice with it? I didn't know which one he preferred.

What did I prefer? Rice. Definitely rice.

I put a casserole with water on to boil, and I put a dash of oil in the frying pan and started chopping up everything I'd need for the salad while I waited for the pan to get warm.

Charo whined behind me and I turned to him with a smile.

"I'm making him dinner, Charo. Isn't there a saying about the way to a man's heart is through his stomach?"

Charo only whined again, his tail wagging half-heartedly from where he was lying next to the kitchen table.

I turned away from him with a smile.

I could only hope it'd be so easy.

PART III
LEAD YOU DOWN MY
BROKEN LINE

JØRGEN

CHAPTER 9

I parked my car with a feeling between dread and actual excitement.

This was a new feeling for me. When had I ever had anything to be excited about? I couldn't remember *ever* being excited. I could feel good about something, but that was as far up as my emotions tended to go.

Yet here I was, parked outside his house, nervous, but still looking forward to seeing him again.

There was no use dawdling, so I got out.

The cold air hit me and I huddled a bit in my jacket as I bent back in to get my gloves. We were going out with the dog later, so this way I wouldn't have to go back to the car.

I locked it, pocketed my keys, and hurried up the

steps. I rang the doorbell and instantly heard barking inside.

But no one came to open it.

I frowned and rang it again. More barking from inside.

The barking wasn't coming from just the other side of the door. It was further away, from inside.

Fuck it all.

I tried the door and it swung inwards. There was still no dog to come greet me, even if he continued to bark.

I could smell something burning.

I went to the kitchen without even taking off my shoes.

What greeted me brought me up short.

Geir was on the floor, out cold. Charo was also on the floor, and Geir's head and neck was resting on his flank.

I stepped over them to shut off the cooker. I also pushed the frying pan and the casseroles aside to minimise the smoke coming from the burnt food.

With the danger of smoke out of the way, I crouched down.

Charo looked at me, tongue hanging out as he panted.

I put my palm on Geir's chest.

It rose and fell slowly.

He was sleeping deeply.

It must've been a little while since he'd had the seizure.

I looked at Charo. He looked benign now, but he might go into protect mode if I were to lift Geir up.

I stroked his head.

"Did you catch him when he fell? Good boy." I rubbed his neck and scratched behind his ears. "Good, good boy. I'm going to carry him to bed now, all right?"

I reached for Geir tentatively, slipping one arm under his neck and the other under his knees.

The dog lay still. He only looked at me with those big, dark eyes.

I lifted Geir up and held him close. I put his head on my shoulder so it wouldn't loll uncomfortably, then I turned to search for his room. Downstairs there was only the kitchen and the living room, plus a bathroom and the hall, so I headed upstairs.

Another bathroom, what must have been his father's room, then finally... Geir's bedroom.

I put him down atop the sheets, then dragged them out from underneath him so I could cover him with them.

He didn't even stir once.

I stared down at him once I straightened up. He was so young. To think that he had to live in fear of having a seizure all the time. That he felt like an outsider because of it and that no one wanted to be friends with him, again because of his epilepsy. It wasn't right.

Charo had padded upstairs after me, and now he put his head onto the mattress. I reached out to ruffle his fur. "You were such a good boy, looking after him back there."

Some of Geir's hair stuck up oddly, and I reached down to sort it out. It was soft, devoid of any styling products.

I pulled back once I realised what I was doing.

I shouldn't touch him.

But he sure was beautiful.

Was it wrong of me to feel that way about him?

It was wrong of me to feel anything for anyone, wasn't it? I couldn't expect someone to deal with me and my issues. Certainly not someone as sweet as him.

Yet I couldn't stay away. I gravitated towards him like there was no one else. And there really wasn't. He was the only one I'd ever felt this way about. How could I possibly stay away when he was the only one who ever made me feel good?

I felt calmer, more relaxed when he was around.

I'd noticed it particularly the night before. Only he could've got me to go to the cinema. I had been prepared to tell him no, going to the cinema was *not* a good idea for me, but seeing his eyes water and hearing him say *I just want a friend* had worn down all my defences.

So I'd gone, and I'd been tense through the whole film, but I'd survived sitting in a dark room, close to him. I wouldn't have got through that film in one piece if there had been more people, if people had been cluttered around me. Then I would've experienced either a flashback or a panic attack, but he being next to me had kept me grounded.

He kept me grounded.

After one last lingering look down at Geir, I went back downstairs.

Charo stayed upstairs, which was good. If Geir woke up it would be a comfort to have his dog there.

I finally got out of my boots and winter jacket, then headed into the kitchen to clean up. I needed to scrub the casseroles clean with steel wool, and even then it was difficult to get them entirely clean. Especially the one with the burnt rice. The frying pan was easier, but the chicken filets couldn't be saved.

The only thing salvageable was the bowl of salad.

When I'd cleaned up, I opened the fridge to see what else Geir might have. He'd need food when he woke up. He'd wanted to make it, for himself and for me, but I was going to do it now.

I was going to make something for him. He deserved it. What he didn't deserve was having a seizure right in the middle of cooking.

I wasn't much of a cook. The food I prepared for myself wasn't exactly extraordinary. The simpler it was, the more likely I was to prepare it. I closed the fridge again. If he felt up to it later, I'd take him out to eat. If not… well, then I guessed I had to scrounge something together.

After drying up the casserole dishes I'd cleaned, I put them in their appropriate places. I took the rubbish out and replaced the bag. The salad couldn't stand out on the counter, so I wrapped some cling film around it, after searching several different drawers, and put it back in the fridge.

Charo came trotting into the kitchen. His wagging tail caught my attention, and when I turned to him he started going in circles before he went back out the door.

I followed him curiously. Maybe he needed to go outside?

But when I saw him standing at the bottom of the stairs, looking at me and then up, I knew it was Geir.

Was something wrong?

I took the stairs two at a time, worried now that maybe he was having more seizures. If he had another seizure now, so shortly after the last one, I'd have to ring for an ambulance.

But there was nothing wrong as far as I could see when I stepped into the room, except for the tear-filled eyes that met mine.

"What's wrong?" My heart beat a mile a minute and I needed to calm down before I suffered an anxiety attack. He was *fine*. Physically, at least.

"I-I'm s-sorry." Geir averted his gaze as he struggled with his tears. "I just wanted to make a nice dinner, and I ruined it all."

"You didn't ruin it." I went over to sit on the edge of his bed. My heart still beat too fast, but the sight of him awake and well calmed me little by little. "You had a seizure. That wasn't your fault."

He didn't say anything, but his sniffles told me everything I needed to know.

He was devastated and I felt for him. He'd tried to do something nice, only for it to end up a disaster.

I reached out tentatively to brush his cheek. It was weird, touching someone like this, but his skin was soft. I liked feeling it, just as I had that first time in the take-away shop. Soft and warm, and quite frankly appealing, something I wouldn't mind doing again.

His head turned back to me at my gesture, his

eyes wide. The green irises were exceptionally brilliant thanks to the tears still swimming in his eyes.

"Don't worry about it. Everything that matters is that you're all right. Food can be thrown away. You just buy new food. But if you'd got hurt..." I shook my head. I didn't want to even *think* about that. He was so sweet, so innocent. *Nothing* could happen to him.

He blinked slowly. "You'd care if I got hurt?"

"Didn't I tell you last night that I would?"

He rubbed his eyes. "I'm sorry. I'm still groggy."

"Go back to sleep. If you feel like it when you wake up again, I'll take you out to dinner. If you don't, I can make something, but I can't promise it'll be anything fancy."

That brought that sweet smile back to his lips. "Thank you."

His fingers wrapped around my hand, which was still holding his. I gave an involuntary jerk—it was second nature to me by now—but I didn't pull away. I couldn't.

"Could you take Charo for a walk?" he asked. "I haven't been out with him since this morning."

I nodded. "I will. Where do you usually take him?" Geir needed his rest. I could tell he was struggling to keep his eyes open.

"The usual trail. Or the folk park. Either or, really,

though I do prefer the trail." Geir's fingers squeezed my hand a bit tighter. "I'm not really sure I'll be up for going out. But if you stop by the shop and buy some more chicken filets, we could make what I had originally planned."

I nodded. "I'll do that."

"We can go out another time?" He looked up at me hopefully.

"Of course we can." I was secretly happy not to go out to eat. Sitting in a restaurant that might be crowded with people… not such a good thing for me.

I started pulling my hand back, and he seemed unwilling to let go of it at first, but he eventually released me. His arm fell limply to the bed and I could tell how he was fighting to stay awake.

"Sleep for a couple of hours now, okay? Charo and I will go out for a long walk, then we'll have that dinner when we get back."

"Thank you," he said, his voice fainter. "I don't know what I would've done today without you."

His eyes shut, and I sat there watching him until his breathing evened out.

I took Charo with me downstairs, where I found his leash on the small table in the hallway. His tail started wagging excitedly as I bundled up in my jacket and laced up my boots. I put the leash on him, grabbed my gloves, then opened the door. I stopped outside, and then I went back in to grab the keys that had been next to the leash. I didn't like leaving him alone, especially with the door unlocked.

So I locked it, pocketed the keys, pulled my gloves on, and looked down at the wagging dog.

"Ready for a walk, boy?"

His tail wagged faster, which I took for a yes, and when I started down the stairs he jumped down ahead of me.

I chose to take him with me to the trail off the graveyard. It was a nice walk, even if it was starting to darken. It was freezing out, but by walking, I kept warm. Charo wasn't concerned about the cold at all, just trotting happily a few paces ahead of me.

I already knew Geir let him go loose on the trail, but he was Geir's dog, not mine, so I didn't dare do the same. I kept him on the leash but gave him as much room to move as possible. He was well trained and didn't jerk the leash at all. If he walked as far away as he could on the leash, he'd stop to wait for me until he once again had space to move.

It was nice to simply stroll along the path with a dog for company. They were the perfect pets, weren't they? Big, furry, reliable, loyal. Always there for you. Never judging you. What more could a person ask for?

Maybe that was the answer.

I only had myself to worry about, and I did that plenty. It would be nice to have someone in my life, even if it was only a dog. It was good companionship. It wouldn't hurt me, or leave me alone with grief. A dog was safe.

We took the long way out of habit. I didn't even think about cutting over to the short way; I automatically turned down the long trail and so did Charo. The trees were denser on the last part of the trail, so it was even darker around us, but once we came out from the gravel road leading back up to the graveyard, it was a bit lighter again. It was February, and darkness fell early at this time of year, but at least I could see what was ahead of me now.

Charo stopped often to sniff on trees or bushes or grass, as well as to relieve himself.

I didn't mind.

I was relaxed and I was content.

It was a lot more than I usually tended to feel. Normally it felt like I was crawling out of my skin from anxiety.

My eyes fell to the side as we started up the graveyard.

Eventually, I tugged a bit on Charo's leash and he followed me willingly across to the parallel road.

It didn't take me long to find the right grave. I'd

been there several times, though usually I felt it was best for my psyche to simply avoid it.

Not today, though. Today I felt more relaxed than I'd been in ages.

It was time to visit Kay's grave again.

CHAPTER 10

*O*nce I stopped in front of the stone, Charo sat down willingly, like he knew we'd be there a while.

I patted his head as I crouched down, then I brushed some snow away from Kay's name. I had paid for this headstone, with the money my own parents were ordered to pay me after the trial.

I'd done it because I'd been the only person Kay had.

In the end, I hadn't been enough.

He'd been too damaged to be able to rely on only one person. Up till now I'd thought I was too damaged as well, but at the moment... Maybe I had it in me to survive. Maybe I could get something out of my life.

"Hey, Kay." I whispered it, like speaking any louder was a crime.

I didn't think anyone else was around, but if they were I didn't want them to hear what I had to say.

There were no flowers or lights in front of Kay's grave, like there was in front of many others, and that was a testament to my not being there for a very long time.

I should buy something for him, something nice. But I'd wait for the snow to melt away first.

"I think I've finally found someone, Kay, someone who's worth it." I bent forward to rest my forehead against the cold black stone.

All Kay had ever wanted was for me to be happy. He'd known I couldn't be with him, which he had told me before he'd—

I guess I'd known it, too, but I had wanted it to be him back then. Maybe because he'd been the only one to give me the time of day. Because he was the only one who'd understood the hell I'd been through, simply because his hell had been so much worse.

I couldn't even imagine.

I couldn't deal with my own childhood.

To imagine what he'd had to go through... just the thought was enough to reduce me into a trembling ball of flashbacks and anxiety.

I couldn't let that happen now.

I'd freeze to death out here if I let that happen, and I had Charo to worry about. He was Geir's best friend and if anything happened to him because of me...

I rubbed at my eyes as I stood up. I could feel my knees protesting after being crouched down in the cold.

Charo looked up at me, happy and unaware of the hell I'd been through before I'd met Kay, and the hell I'd been through after.

"Let's go to the shop. Then we'll go home." I scratched behind his ears, which had Charo's tail wagging again.

We started back up the road. We passed right by the church, which looked eerie in the dark.

It took us about twenty minutes to reach the grocery shop, and I secured Charo's leash around the ring intended for dogs outside before going in. This wasn't usually the shop I went to, but it was the one closest to Geir's home. Still, I was familiar with it, and I was all set on taking the route past the vegetable section when I caught sight of someone I definitely did *not* want to meet.

I did a double take, anxiety curling through me at coming face to face with them, and found my way to the fridge.

I checked the date on the chicken filets quickly,

chose the one that looked best, then quickly went back up to the tills. The quicker I was out of there, the less possibility there was of meeting them.

Today was not my lucky day, because when I exited the store, there they were. Standing almost directly in front of Charo. Charo stood up when he saw me and he wagged his tail. I glanced at him, glanced at them, and then inched my way over to the dog, hoping they wouldn't catch sight of me.

"Jørgen!"

I undid the knot around the ring before I turned to face them. I didn't want to. I didn't have any problems with Christina on my own, but Jo... I couldn't really deal with Jo alone, and especially not when he was in our cousin's company.

"Hey."

I clutched at the leash in one hand and the plastic bag in the other, needing something to ground me. I could feel both their eyes on me. They both had blue eyes, Jo's pale so much like my own and Christina's piercing and clear.

"Who's the dog?" Christina asked. Her voice was normal, not hostile, not overly friendly. It was simply curious.

"It's just a dog," I murmured, looking down at Charo. He was so much more than that, but it wasn't something I wanted *them* to know about.

Awkward silence descended.

Jo and I had grown up together, but we'd never been close. Whereas I'd been smack in the middle of hell, he'd been on the outside, all safe and happy by himself and not subjected to the nightmare my childhood had been.

Christina… She was our cousin and I liked her well enough. I just didn't really *know* her. But then I didn't really *know* anyone, did I? Not even my own extended family.

"It's been a while," Christina said tentatively, like she didn't know what to say or how I'd react. Maybe it was both. "How've you been?"

"Good." I dared to look up and my eyes zeroed in on Jo's hand placed confidently on the small of Christina's back. Something tightened around my chest, and I suddenly had difficulty breathing. "I have to go." I tugged Charo with me, making a big circle around them, then I walked as fast I could without outright running.

"Jørgen!" It was Christina who called after me, not Jo.

It was never Jo.

My chest hurt, my heart beat irregularly.

I was trembling.

And sweating.

I was having a panic attack and it was happening

right out in the open where anyone could see me.

My hand trembled so badly when I unlocked Geir's front door that I didn't think I'd manage it.

I did, though, and once the door was open, I stepped inside and slammed it closed behind me.

I dropped the plastic bag and Charo's leash, then slid to the floor, where I bent in on myself.

It felt like I was choking.

I was short of breath and nauseous and my mind flooded with everything I fought to push away, everything I kept buried.

Everything I couldn't deal with.

My uncle's sneer as he came into my room.

His belt, the one he always wore with the big metal buckle that would crack down on my skin if I didn't do as he said, if I didn't lie still.

His fists, which beat me into a bloody pulp, beat me until I couldn't even feel the pain anymore, until I was unconscious, thoughtless—until he could do anything he wanted to me without me struggling against him.

Groans of pleasure as he forced his way inside me, the smell of his sweat, his coarse body hair rubbing against my skin, his semen trickling down my thighs when he was done.

His big, broad, *soft* body squishing me into the bed during and after.

My screams of pain and hopelessness and sheer terror.

No one ever heard, no one ever cared.

No one ever did anything to help me.

They left my uncle to do whatever he wanted to me.

"Jørgen?" Someone touched me and I flinched away.

"No, no, no, no, no, no." I pressed my forehead against my knees to the point of pain. My cheeks were wet.

"Jørgen, you're scaring me—"

That voice…

That voice was familiar.

There was no pain with that voice.

That voice did not belong in my childhood, it was newer than that.

It belonged to someone I cared about, someone who'd been nothing but kind to me.

Geir!

I lifted my head slowly to find him on his knees in front of me.

Charo's head stuck out from behind Geir's back. The sight of the two pushed my childhood nightmares away, brought me back to the here and now.

I was still short of breath. My heart still beat like mad, I was still sweating and nauseous, and my chest was still tight. But the flashbacks had disappeared, and they were the most difficult to deal with.

"Too hot." I pulled the zipper of my jacket down and wrenched it off. I was still sweating, and I pulled at my jumper. That one wasn't as easy, with my disorientation and the panic attack still riding me.

"Let me help you." Another pair of hands pulled at my jumper, and I finally got it over my head.

Blessedly cool air hit my skin, snaking down the collar of my tee and cooling the sweat.

My trembling slowly subsided, along with the heavy sweating, and though my chest still felt tight and I had difficulty breathing, I was slowly starting to feel better.

Geir stayed on his knees, his gaze calmly locked on me as I tried my best to calm myself down.

He pushed Charo away when he tried to slip around him to get to me, and for that I was grateful. I didn't want to be touched at the moment, not even by the dog.

"I'm sorry," I managed to get out eventually. "You shouldn't have seen that."

"What happened?" He didn't seem to be freaked out, just worried. I'd never seen anyone have a panic attack or flashback before, but I supposed it couldn't be a pretty sight.

"Panic attack," I told him quietly. "It was a panic attack."

"The door woke me up, but when Charo came upstairs with his leash still on and trying his best to get me to follow him back downstairs—" His tongue flicked out to wet his lips. "I didn't know what to do once I saw you. You seemed to be having some sort of breakdown, like you were in physical pain, and I just— I didn't know what to do."

I hated putting him through my issues. He shouldn't have been subjected to it. "I'm sorry."

"Don't be." He bent forward a bit, his gaze still locked on mine. "Don't be sorry for this, Jørgen. I was worried about you because I didn't know *what* was going on. If I'd known it was a panic attack, and if I'd known what to do to help you through that, I would've gladly done it."

I looked into his clear green eyes. They were so sincere.

"I met my brother and my cousin at the shop," I said.

He tilted his head to the side slightly. "How is that cause for a panic attack?"

"They're together." By just saying the words, I could feel my chest squeeze a bit tighter.

"Your brother and your cousin? Is she his cousin as well?"

TT KOVE

I nodded. "It's legal. I know they're willing, I do, that they're not f-forcing each other. I know, rationally, that they just want to be together. But it's still family, and it's not far from cousin and cousin to uncle and nephew, and I just can't deal with it." I rubbed at my face. The tears had stopped a while ago, but I knew I must look horribly blotchy and red eyed. "I can't."

I could hear Geir swallow. "Can I hug you?"

I looked up at him at that. "Why?"

"Because I don't know what else to do." He smiled sadly at me. "I want to make you feel better, but I don't know how. I know you don't like being touched, but hugs always make *me* feel better. Maybe it will for you too, once you get used to it."

I could only nod, and he bent further forward so he could slide his arms around my shoulders. His smooth cheek rested against my slightly stubbled one, and that simple tender gesture was almost my undoing.

I wrapped my arms around him and clung to him.

It was so different from our previous hug, where I'd been so hesitant. Now I wasn't. Now all I wanted was someone to hold on to, someone who wouldn't hurt me or leave me all by myself to deal with everything.

Geir would never do that.

The tightness around my chest slowly dissipated, but I didn't let go of him. He felt good, he felt safe. I knew I would have to leave, though, because I was drenched in sweat.

I needed a shower badly, and so I forced myself to pull away from him. I did it very hesitantly.

"I should leave."

"No." He shook his head as he sat back. "I'm making dinner and you're taking a shower. And then we're going to eat together."

I looked up at him. His jaw was clenched in determination.

"I haven't got anything to change into." I suspected it wasn't a very good excuse. I didn't want to leave, but at the same time I had to shower and at least change my T-shirt.

"I'll find something of my dad's." He rested his hands on his knees and he chewed on his bottom lip. "Please don't go. I don't want you to leave."

I didn't want to leave either, so I nodded.

"Okay. I'll stay."

CHAPTER 11

*G*eir had remade the ruined dinner by the time I came back downstairs.

I wore one of his dad's tees, which was too large on me, but at least it was a garment that wasn't soaked in my sweat.

Geir had set the table for two and everything seemed to be ready. He turned to me with a smile as I stepped across the threshold.

"I could've helped you," I murmured.

"I wanted to do this for you today. I was going to have it all done before you showed up. Then my seizure ruined it all. I'm feeling okay now, while you're not, so I could finally do the one thing I originally did want to do for you."

Panic attacks and flashbacks, as well as anxiety

attacks, left me emotional, and what he said had me swallowing hard to dislodge the big lump that suddenly stuck in my throat.

No one ever did something for me.

I was alone, I'd always been alone.

I had extensive family, of course, but I'd never been close to them. My childhood… well. I'd never forged the bonds with them that they had with each other.

"Sit down." Geir pointed at the chair closest to me. "Let's eat."

I did as commanded, and he sat down opposite me.

We piled our plates with chicken, rice, sauce, and salad in silence. It wasn't an uncomfortable silence. It was actually quite nice to just sit there without feeling the need to say something. The food was warm and tasted good. It was great to finally have a proper home cooked meal.

"Jørgen… can I ask you something? Something personal?"

"Sure." He'd seen me at my most personal, right in the middle of a panic attack and flashback. Couldn't really get more personal than that, could it?

"Those scars… What happened?"

I lifted my head to stare at him for several tense, loaded seconds, then I dropped my eyes to stare at my bare forearms. Thick, long scars ran up them from wrist to elbow.

"I tried to kill myself."

That had certainly been a low point, hadn't it?

It hadn't even worked.

I had wanted to die when I'd done it. I'd even taken pills in case the cutting hadn't worked, but I'd been found before they could work properly. I couldn't blame Tarjei for calling for an ambulance. He had stuck with me all my life; of course he wasn't going to let me die.

"Was it related to what you told me earlier?" Geir's voice was hesitant. He didn't know how I would react to the questions, so I could understand that.

"It was related to so much, and that was included, yes." I met his eyes. "You have no idea how much it was related to."

Geir's Adam's apple bobbed as he swallowed, and he dropped his head. He took a couple of more bites of food, chewing slowly.

This wasn't a subject I was comfortable with, and this close to a panic attack I didn't want to take the change of plummeting right back into another one. So I searched around for another topic of conversation. "Have you used your gift card yet?"

"No." Another bite of food, head still bowed.

"There's only one shop, perhaps two, where I may find some clothes I like, but they don't really have much to choose from."

I knew what that was like. Our town wasn't the biggest, and the shops reflected that.

An idea popped into my mind. "How would you feel about going to the biggest shopping centre in the county? Must be easier to find something nice when there's a hundred and seventy shops to choose from."

Geir finally lifted his head, expression surprised. "But... That's a three hour drive away. Maybe longer."

"Yeah. And?" I smiled crookedly. "I've got a car."

His lips parted. "When would we go? It takes a whole day."

"Maybe this weekend? Saturday?"

I wanted to get out of town and I wanted to take him with me.

I liked spending time with him. Going away for the day seemed like a splendid idea, even if we would be going to a shopping centre.

That idea left me anxious, but it was something he wanted to do and I wanted him to be happy.

We wouldn't meet anyone we knew there anyway. If we did we would be extremely unlucky. Or I would be, but that was the story of my life.

Still, simple strangers must be easier than being in this town, where there was always the danger of meeting someone familiar, someone tied into all my bad memories.

Geir smiled shyly. "Yeah, I would— I would really like that."

Surprisingly, so would I.

∼

SATURDAY ARRIVED with bright sun and melting snow. The wind was chilly, but other than that it was a very nice day.

I sat in the driver's seat in my jumper, having folded my jacket in the back seat.

Geir sat in the passenger seat, also in his jumper. He'd put his jacket on top of mine when I'd picked him up.

Charo was resting in the backseat. I'd told Geir to bring him, since we would be spending the entire day on our trip.

Geir had brought his sketchbook, and when we weren't talking, he drew in it. His fingers, long and slender, gripped the pencil and made long, swift strokes over the blank paper. The hem of his jumper inched up the more he drew, and I frowned slightly at the bracelet he was wearing.

"What's that?" I asked as I turned my eyes back to the road.

"What?"

"That bracelet."

"It's my SOS bracelet."

I glanced over to see Geir running a finger over the flat surface of the bracelet.

"I wasn't wearing it that day we first met. But I found it in a drawer, so I thought I should start wearing it again. You never know, next time I have a seizure you might not be around."

"What's the purpose of it?" I couldn't remember my uncle ever wearing such a bracelet.

"It opens and inside there's basic information about epilepsy. I also have an information card in my wallet that looks like a bank card. The front has info about what to do when I have a seizure. First aid and stuff. I don't know if you saw it when you went through my wallet?"

"I didn't." I'd only been interested in the bank card, to find his name. It hadn't even occurred to me to look after anything else.

"I've got this too."

I looked over to see what Geir was talking about. He was holding up his mobile, with its back to me. It had a white cover with blue heart lines across it. Between the two upper lines, it said *I have epilepsy*.

"That's nice."

"I know, right?" Geir turned it around to look at it himself. "Dad got it for me last year, after he gave me my new mobile for Christmas."

"Your dad's gone a lot. Is that okay with you?"

If they had a normal family relation, I imagined it would have been.

I didn't know what normal was, not really. The most normal I'd experienced was Tarjei's parents or my uncle Thomas, but I'd never lived with them. I'd been living in hell until I'd been old enough to live by myself. Well, except for a short stint with Grandma, anyway.

"Yeah, I guess. He only wants for us to live comfortably. I can't really blame him for that. It's his job, his education. If he quit, what would he do? Dad really likes his job. Besides, I'm old enough to take care of myself."

"That you are." I chanced another glance over at him and smiled.

He blinked once, then he smiled back.

His smile was absolutely stunning. I couldn't say no to that smile. Whenever it was directed at me, I couldn't even think of anything else.

We were lucky enough that the ferry was there and boarding when we arrived, so we didn't have to wait.

We left Charo in the car once I'd parked and headed inside, where I insisted on buying us both something to eat for an early lunch. We ended up with a bread roll each, both with salad, ham and cheese, cucumber, and red peppers.

"I really appreciate this," Geir said once we'd sat down. "You, this trip, everything."

I wondered what *everything* meant.

Maybe everything we'd done since we'd first met. Or the fact that I'd walked Charo with him for the past three evenings, as well as had dinner with him. What could I say? I enjoyed his company. Much more than I'd ever enjoyed *anyone's* company before.

Even Tarjei's.

"When you said to me that you only wanted a friend…" I stopped, not quite sure how to continue. I knew his eyes were on me, though. "Maybe that's what I wanted too. A friend." Someone who would understand me.

I loved Tarjei, I did, but he didn't understand what it was like to be me sometimes. Tarjei was social, popular, and he'd never had a problem adapting to anything.

Sometimes that could be quite frustrating.

Even if he'd been there through it all, he couldn't quite understand what was going through my mind. How *hard* it was to deal with everything.

I had a feeling Geir understood the little I'd let slip a lot more, and that he had more sympathy with being different, since he was an outcast as well.

"I was perfectly happy being all alone, but you— you changed that." He'd changed it so bloody fast I hadn't even seen it coming. He'd managed to get me to the cinema, something I'd never even done with Tarjei.

"I'm glad to hear that. You changed things for me too, you know. I finally have someone I can talk to, someone who won't ridicule me, or trip me when I walk past them, or yell slurs after me. Someone who understands my epilepsy and actually knows what to do when I have a seizure." He fiddled with his forkful of salad while he said all that, but I could tell he was sincere.

Sincere, but embarrassed, which was why he wasn't looking at me.

"Is it really bad at school?" I wanted to do something to make his situation better, but what could I do? *I* wasn't in school, I couldn't be there for him. All I could do was be there when he was done, and hope that his classmates didn't completely break his spirit.

"I don't like school anymore. I used to be excited about it, because I finally got to do art, but not anymore. Jonas is so cruel to me, and the rest of them just fall in line behind him... I don't know what I've done wrong. I don't know why they can't think for themselves, why they have to follow him around, like he's the king. He may act like it, but he's *not*."

"If he thinks he's king now, just imagine what real life will be for him when school's over." I'd had a couple of people like Jonas in my class too, though they'd never bothered me. I didn't know what had happened to them, however, because I didn't give a shit. I'd always had enough dealing with myself and my issues to think about random people.

"Yeah, maybe that's true." He seemed to perk up a bit, so he might have actually believed it.

I leaned forward a bit so I could look at him closer. "If he goes too far... you are allowed to hit back. You know that, right? You don't have to take everything. He's the one in the wrong, he's the one bothering you, making your life hell. So you are allowed to fight back."

Geir bit nervously on his lower lip. "He's bigger than me, and stronger. I've got nothing against him. I'm small and skinny and I haven't got any muscles. Not compared to him, anyway."

Well, he had a point. He wasn't the biggest bloke around. "Do you work out?"

He shook his head. "When I was younger, I wasn't even part of gym class because they believed physical exertion would trigger seizures. It's just a myth, but I don't think Dad's got it yet. He doesn't want me lifting heavy objects or being part of gym, really. I mean, I *am* part of gym class now, but if I feel tired I'm allowed to just walk away. Gym's not really my favourite either, you know, because Jonas is there and he's as he's usually like. So I tend to just watch and not participate, so I can go change before he comes in."

I nodded that I understood. I'd been excused from gym as well back in my school days, but that hadn't been because of bullying, but because I couldn't handle changing around all my classmates or coming into physical contact with them out in the gym.

There'd been many a time I'd broken down in a full-blown panic attack at school. Maybe that's why everyone had left me alone; I was the mental freak. I'd heard those words used sometimes, but I'd never cared much about them.

The conductor stopped by our table and I handed him my debit card. I could feel Geir's eyes on me the whole time, and once the conductor continued on, I turned to him with raised eyebrows. "What?"

"You don't have to keep paying for me," he said. "You paid for breakfast, and now for the ferry. I can pay for myself, you know."

"I know. I just don't mind paying. It's my car. I

suggested this trip. So I pay for these expenses." I smiled to take the sting off my words.

I didn't mind paying. I never used my money on anything but rent, electricity, and food. I had a lot more money than he did, since he still lived at home with his dad and didn't work to earn his own money.

Someone bumped into me and I jerked away, further in towards the window. My head swivelled around to see who it had been, and I found a small child blinking at me before he barrelled away towards his parents.

The damage was done, though. My skin crawled and all the talking inside the cafeteria was getting to me, making me antsy.

It was pathetic that a small child could set me off.

"Should we go back to the car?" I stood up, not really giving Geir an option. I couldn't stay anymore. We'd been in our own little bubble, but it had burst open the moment that child had bumped into me.

"Are you all right?" Geir looked at me anxiously, but I didn't answer him. I couldn't. I had to get to my car.

I clicked the key and almost dove into the driver's seat.

Charo sat up excitedly in the back seat, but I couldn't deal with him.

I put my forehead down on the steering wheel

and breathed in deeply. Why had I suggested this trip at all? I knew I couldn't deal with crowds, and it was a bloody *Saturday*. The shopping centre would be more crowded than any other day in the week.

It was mental.

But it was also the only day we could both go. He had school on weekdays and I had work. I just wanted him to have one good day, where he wouldn't have to worry about all the bullies at school —and here I was ruining it.

I managed to push the oncoming panic attack away by breathing in deeply several times. This was for him. I had to do it for him. He was worth the discomfort; he was worth having to deal with it.

When I finally sat back in the seat, I was still feeling antsy, but I had myself mostly under control.

"If you want to go back home, we can," Geir said quietly next to me. "I won't mind."

Of course he would mind. He'd been looking forward to our trip.

I'd spent every evening with him since he'd had his seizure, and I could *tell* that he was excited about this trip.

I would have to deal, because this was for him.

It wasn't about me at all, it was all for him.

"It's okay." My voice sounded steadier than I'd thought it would. "I'm okay."

"Are you sure?"

I could tell from his voice that he didn't believe me. "Yeah, I'm sure."

Maybe if I said it often enough *I*'d actually believe it.

CHAPTER 12

*M*y chest felt tight by the time we took the lift up to the first floor of the shopping centre. The first floor was the proper part of the centre, so even before we reached it I wasn't feeling good.

It didn't bode well for the rest of the visit.

Geir kept shooting nervous glances my way, and I hated it.

I hated that he was worried, I hated that there was something to actually worry about, and most of all I hated that I was ruining our trip. We were supposed to have *fun*. He was supposed to have his thoughts on something that wasn't troubling for him, and yet here we were with me barely holding on and him being worried because of it.

As long as no one touched me or came up on me unexpectedly, I reckoned I could deal, though.

Most of the shops were too crowded for me, so whenever Geir disappeared into one I stayed outside to wait for him.

When we walked past a jewellery shop, he stopped for a while to look at a necklace.

"That's really cool," he said as he scratched the back of his neck. "Kind of expensive, though."

He went into a clothing shop next, and I gladly held the small bag he'd got from the previous shop. I leant back against the wall so I could see every-thing that was going on around me while I waited for him. I was trying to think about something else besides the amount of people and the noise, and my mind settled on that necklace he'd been admiring.

I went back to the jeweller shop to look at it prop-erly myself. It was nice, all leather with a yin-yang pendant in front.

A middle-aged woman approached me. "Can I help you?"

"I want that one." I nodded to the necklace.

"Do you want me to wrap it for you?"

"Yes, please." I glanced back to the shop Geir had disappeared into.

No sign of him yet.

I hoped to finish my purchase and be out of the jeweller shop before he was done.

I wanted the necklace to be a surprise for later.

The woman put the necklace in a black box and then wrapped it up in shiny blue paper. She even put a bow on top of it before putting it in a plastic bag. I paid by card, thanked her, and walked out of the shop.

I put the small bag in my inside pocket so Geir wouldn't see it until I decided to give the present to him.

He came out of the shop just before I reached it, and I flashed him a smile as he looked up at me worriedly. He had a big plastic bag in his hand. "You finally found something?"

"Yeah. They've got a lot more to choose from here than they do back home." He smiled back at me. Just the sight of that smile eased some of my anxiety. "Do you want to continue on or do you want to leave?"

"If you've got more to do, we'll stay." This whole trip was for him, after all.

"Don't you want to shop anything, now that we're here?"

I shrugged. "I don't really need anything." The moment I'd said it I realised there was actually something I needed. "Maybe we could head down to look at the sport shops?"

I needed new hiking shoes. My old ones were a bit worn, since I used them a lot during summer.

I liked hiking. It was relaxing for my mind and was my only way of exercise, since I couldn't bear being in a gym.

"Yeah. Let's." Geir nodded enthusiastically.

The sports shop was as crowded as the rest of the centre, but it was a big store, so it didn't give me the same claustrophobic feeling the clothing shops tended to instill in me. We headed to the back of the shop where they had all the shoes.

"I've got hiking boots too. They're from two years ago, I think, but I hardly ever use them, so they look new."

"Why don't you use them?" I looked up at him from where I was examining a pair of Gore-Tex boots. They needed to be sturdy and waterproof, but also comfortable to wear.

"I can't go hiking on my own, not even with Charo." Geir shrugged and looked away. "I can take the public trails around town, of course, but proper hiking... Not alone. I can't take that chance."

That was true. "You should come with me once spring set in. If something happens, I'll take care of you."

His cheeks reddened, but he smiled slightly, so

my words hadn't embarrassed him completely. "Yeah, I'd like that. That would be fun."

"Hiking is excellent for both conditioning and strength." I picked out another pair of boots and examined them closely. They weren't what I was looking for, so I found a third pair I liked enough to try them on.

They fit my feet nicely, and after trying to walk in them, I settled on my purchase. I didn't have much patience for stores on my best days, and especially not when they were crowded and I could all but feel the panic crawling over my skin.

We headed back, because Geir wanted to check out some clothing at the front of the centre, as well as a bookshop. Once again I waited outside while he went into the clothing shop. It was the most crowded one yet, and I couldn't stomach it.

I went over to the banister to look downstairs. People were hurrying in every direction, some alone, some in pairs, some dragging both willing and unwilling children with them. Saturdays were always hectic.

Something caught my attention out of the corner of my eye. I turned around, blinked, then stared after the woman's back as she headed away from me.

I knew, rationally, that it couldn't be her.

It couldn't be my mother, but she'd been so alike her at first glance.

The noise around me disappeared. The real world fell away.

Darkness. Darkness all around me. I knew where I was, of course I knew, but I couldn't see. I couldn't see anything. My cheek throbbed after the slap, my knees hurt after the shove that left me sprawled at the bottom of the basement stairs, and my ears rang after the screaming that had preceded it all.

"Jørgen?"

Someone touched me, someone was there in the darkness, someone could reach me.

I cowered. I couldn't do anything else. I was trapped down in the basement, in total darkness.

"Jørgen?"

It was the same voice that had spoken earlier, but no one touched me anymore.

I knew that voice, I *liked* that voice.

"Jørgen, please. Can you hear me?"

The voice had come from behind me the first time. Now it was in front. But I couldn't see, there was total darkness…

I closed my eyes, took deep breaths.

That voice belonged to Geir.

Geir wasn't part of the basement—he hadn't been in my life then. Geir was in the here and now, and that was where I needed to be. I needed to get back to him.

The first thing that registered as I opened my eyes was the light. Then the bustle of people, and last…

Geir's face, in front of me, looking up at me. His eyes were narrowed, and he chewed on his bottom lip. I'd noticed he did that a lot when he was nervous or worried.

"Jørgen?" His eyes were a bit blank and it made me wonder how long he'd been trying to get in contact with me.

"Yeah. Yeah. I'm here." I bent my head and scratched at the back of my neck. My skin itched. I was definitely feeling antsy now, but my chest hadn't compressed any further and I'd managed to avoid a full-blown panic attack.

I'd say my thanks whenever I could. Having a panic attack right in the middle of a busy shopping centre was not something I wanted to happen.

"What's wrong?"

He took a step closer, into my personal bubble. With anyone else I would've minded, but not with him.

Instead of pushing him away, or stepping away, as I would've done with someone else, I put my hand at the back of his neck and pulled him into a light, loose hug.

He hadn't ever hurt me, and I didn't think he ever would. He was sweet, tried his best, and I trusted him. I trusted him with *this*, something I'd never trust anyone else with. *Physical touch.* Just the thought of it with anyone else left me cold.

"Jørgen? You scared me. I couldn't get you to answer me. You wouldn't look at me. You pulled away when I tried to touch you."

"I had a flashback," I said, quietly so that only he could hear it. "I saw something that reminded me of my past and I had a flashback. It was like that night, you know, except I managed to avoid the panic attack afterwards."

"Why do you keep having flashbacks and panic attacks?" His voice was as low as mine.

He didn't move away from my hug, if anything he leaned a bit more forward, but he didn't grab onto me either. Maybe he was afraid I'd pull away from him again.

"They say I have PTSD," I said. "*They* being a counsellor I saw after—after everything."

"Are you seeing that counsellor now?"

"No. No, I—I'm not." I tried to soften my tone, but I couldn't give him the reason. I couldn't bear to think about it, least of all talk about it. Not without a breakdown, and I couldn't let that happen right now.

Geir didn't say anything, just turned his head

slightly so our cheeks pressed together more. He put his hands hesitantly on my sides, but that only made me pull him in further.

I gave him a long, tight, proper hug before finally releasing him.

His eyes were back to normal when he tilted his head back so I could see him.

"I think we should leave," he said. "I've bought enough clothes. It's time to get out of here."

I didn't have it in me to protest anymore. I'd had enough of crowds for the day.

We took the lift downstairs and headed to the wide sliding doors leading outside. The weather had been nice that morning, but it was grey outside now. It was either going to start to snow or rain. Maybe a storm was coming.

Charo rested peacefully in the back seat when we got to the car. I didn't think I'd ever seen a calmer dog, but that might have a lot to do with the fact that he was old.

He might've been livelier in his youth.

"We could find a place to eat," I suggested. I felt guilty for cutting our day short, even if I was extremely relieved we weren't in the shopping centre anymore.

"You sure?" Geir fished his mobile out of his pocket. "We can make it home before it's too late. I can make something home cooked for us. Just the two of us."

That did sound nice. "It's going to be another three hour drive home."

"I know." He bobbed his head in a nod. "But that's okay, isn't it? If we get hungry we could always stop by a gas station and buy a hotdog or something to tide us over until we get home."

I couldn't argue with his logic.

Besides, a meal cooked at home sounded a lot better than going out to eat. Out meant other people, and I'd had enough of other people for days.

I was a danger to myself and others with people around.

"All right, then." I opened the driver's side. "Let's go home."

PART IV
WE MAKE IT UP AS WE GO

GEIR

CHAPTER 13

Jørgen drove me home once we got back into town.

I didn't want us to part, but I didn't possess the nerve to ask if I could stay over at his flat either.

It wasn't like there was anything between us. We'd only ever hugged, and that was what friends did. That was what I'd asked of him. To be friends.

So home I went.

I didn't bother putting a leash on Charo; I just let him out of the car and he followed me to the front door.

Jørgen had got out from the driver's side and crossed around so that he was now leaning against the passenger side.

I turned to him, not quite sure how to say good-bye. On one hand, I'd asked for us to be friends; on the other hand, he'd taken me away for the whole day. Didn't that hint at something other than friendship between us?

"I did have a nice day today," I told him quietly. "Really, I did." I could tell he didn't believe me, but it was true. Just being in his presence made my day a good day.

He didn't say anything, simply unzipped his jacket and reached inside.

I frowned slightly as he drew out a small bag, then took out a finely wrapped gift and handed it to me.

"I'm really sorry about today. Also, happy belated birthday."

I took the present gingerly. "What is this?" It was wrapped so nicely I almost didn't want to ruin it, but my curiosity got the better of me.

I tried to be as gentle as possible when I ripped it open. The blue paper concealed a black box, and I popped the lid in trepidation. What could he possibly have got me?

I swallowed heavily.

Inside the box nestled the yin-yang necklace I'd looked at.

"This was really expensive!" It fell out of my mouth before I knew what I was saying. I could feel my cheeks heat. "I mean—thank you. Thank you so much!" I took the necklace out of the box so I could look at it properly. It was even nicer up close than it had been on display.

"It wasn't that expensive. Besides, you wanted it. And I wanted to get you something nice."

Could I read more into it? Probably not. Friends could buy each other things, couldn't they?

"Can you put it on me?" I held the necklace out to him, then zipped my jacket down a bit and turned around.

I was glad I wasn't wearing a scarf; I'd figured since we'd be in the car all day, then in a shopping centre, I wouldn't need one.

Jørgen did as asked and put the necklace around my neck. His fingers brushed the back of my neck slightly as he secured the lock. His fingers were cold, but that wasn't why goose bumps popped down my spine.

I turned on the spot.

He looked down at me with an unreadable expression. His lips were parted just the tiniest bit.

I'd never kissed anyone in my life, but I wanted to kiss him.

I bent forward, tilted my head up. It wasn't

enough, so I gingerly put my hands on his neck and drew him down the rest of the way.

He didn't fight it, and soon our lips met in a brush of tentative, unsure union. His lips were soft, so different from the light feel of stubble around them and on his chin.

I wanted to feel them again, so I did. I pressed harder against him this time.

Jørgen didn't move, and I wondered if I'd gone too far. I was about to pull back, make sure I hadn't unwittingly sent him back into another flashback or the start of a panic attack, when he suddenly pulled me in close and kissed me back with a passion I hadn't known how to show.

I wrapped my arms fully around his shoulder and kissed back as much as I was able. This being my first kiss, I was sure it was all kinds of clumsy, but it was good too.

He was good—he was bloody fantastic! Kissing wasn't anything I'd thought much about before, but kissing Jørgen... It was like nothing I'd ever experienced. Our lips slid together, our tongues played lightly, and it was simply a wonderful feeling to be *kissed* by him.

His arms were around me, holding me tight. It was even tighter than the hug he'd given me in the shopping centre, but I didn't complain one bit. I *loved* it. I liked being someone he could hug, because I suspected he didn't get nearly enough of them from anyone else. Hugs were great.

Kissing him was better, though.

When he stopped kissing me, my heart raced and I struggled to regain my breathing.

He let his head fall to my shoulder.

"That was my first kiss," I whispered against his neck. "My very first kiss."

"Believe it or not, but it was mine too."

That piece of information left me reeling. He'd never kissed anyone before? Handsome, gorgeous Jørgen hadn't been *kissed*? *I* was his first. I was his first kiss! We'd been each other's first kiss. What were the odds?

"I really like you, Jørgen. I like you more than a friend. A lot more."

I could hear him swallow. "Me too, but…"

"But we can't be together?"

He finally pulled back from me, but he didn't step away. Instead he looked at me, somber and sad. "You do realise that I have a lot of issues?"

"Yeah. But that doesn't matter. I just want to be with you."

He stared at me, glanced away, looked back at me, then cast his gaze around us as if looking for something to focus on that wasn't me. "Maybe I want that too, but… slowly?"

I nodded. If he wanted us to go slow, that was fine with me.

Maybe even preferable.

I'd never had a relationship with anyone, so I didn't know what it entailed. Taking it slow would ensure we would both be comfortable.

"I can do slow. I don't mind slow at all. I'm just happy that you would actually want to be with me." My cheeks burned in embarrassment.

"Why wouldn't I? You're wonderful, Geir. Just… wonderful."

I could tell he was embarrassed, and it made me smile. I reached up to run a hand over his cheek without thinking, but for once he didn't flinch away from me when I initiated contact.

"If there is something, Jørgen, you can tell me. Like with touching and stuff. If there's some things I shouldn't do, some things that trigger you." His stubble rasped my palm. It was ticklish. He couldn't have shaved today, maybe not yesterday either.

"I don't know… Don't touch me if I'm having a flashback or a panic attack. Not without asking, anyway. Don't ever come upon me from behind without me knowing you're there. That can lead to nasty… things."

"I'll be careful." I didn't like the look in his eyes when he talked about this. They were sad, yes, but there was something even deeper than simple sadness in them. I didn't like it at all.

"Also, if I am having a panic attack or flashback, talking to me helps. Talk about anything, the surroundings maybe, or do something to ground me. I don't know. Usually I ride it out alone, but if you're there... You calmed me down today. Normally I would've gone right over to a panic attack, but that didn't happen at the centre. That's because of you."

I'd actually been of some help, or comfort, to him?

I hadn't known what to do, so I'd just kept on rambling. It must have actually worked. I was glad.

I vividly remembered the panic attack I'd witnessed, and it hadn't been fun. During the flash-back, he'd been distant. I hadn't been able to get him to look at me or talk to me. It had been like he was in a completely different place.

He probably had been, in his mind.

But the panic attack... He seemed like he'd been in such agony. It had been heartbreaking to witness.

"I'm glad I was of some help to you." It was all I could think to say. What else could I say? I *was* glad he'd found some help in me.

"So... slowly?" He bent his head to look at the

ground. "Let's not define anything and just—just stay the way we are and see where it leads. You have to know that I'm not a very good candidate for any kind of relationship."

"Yes, you are. You just have a bit more to deal with than most." I reached out to touch his hand. Now that we'd actually kissed, I felt like I could touch him more too. "And yeah, we'll take it slowly. We'll see what happens."

He smiled then, and I couldn't stop staring. He was gorgeous whenever, but when he smiled he was stunning.

"You should smile more often," I said. "It's a good look on you."

He seemed taken aback, but the smile stayed in place. "I could say the same thing about you."

I retracted my hand to press against my own hot cheeks. Compliments were nice, but they also made me feel self-conscious.

Charo pushed his nose against my thigh.

"I guess I should get inside." I didn't want to leave him. I wanted to stay right there, screw the cold and the darkness and everything. I didn't want this moment to end.

"Go get some sleep." Jørgen bent down to pat Charo on the head. When he straightened again, his eyes were on me. "I had a nice day with you, even if my issues made a mess of things."

"I think, in the future, we should stay away from crowded shopping centres. Crowded places in general. I'm looking forward to the hiking trips you've promised me."

"Me too." I could tell he hesitated about something... and then he quickly leaned forward and pecked me on the lips. "Good night."

I unwillingly took a step back. I didn't want our moment to end, but it was late and it was cold.

"Good night, Jørgen."

One thing was for certain, though, and that was that I would definitely be seeing him again.

We weren't boyfriends, not exactly, but we were so much more than friends now.

CHAPTER 14

I sat at my desktop, steering the mouse with one hand while the other held a frozen package of vegetables to my eye and cheek.

My skin throbbed on that side, but the frozen package helped.

It was all Jonas' fault. He'd been his usual nasty self at school, but when he'd tried to trip me, I'd finally found some latent piece of courage and spoken back to him. It had all ended with him hitting me, and now here I was with a package of frozen vegetables pressed to the right side of my face.

I had several tabs on flashbacks and panic attacks open on my desktop. I'd tried to do as much research as possible since our trip to the shopping centre three weeks ago, and I thought I had a good grasp on what to do now if Jørgen suffered one or both in front of me again. He'd had a panic attack a week ago, but it had been almost over by the time I'd come over to his flat.

We'd spent almost every evening together since.

I'd had my winter holiday the week after our trip, but Jørgen had been working so I'd spent my days alone with Charo.

The evenings, though... they were spent with him. They really couldn't be spent in better company.

Nothing much had happened between us since.

He didn't jerk away as violently when I tried to touch him now, which was nice, but we hadn't gone further either.

I didn't mind it, as he obviously needed to take things slow. If even half of the stuff I'd guessed about was right, I knew I could never push him. That could lead to pushing him away completely. That was not a scenario I ever wanted to happen.

Jørgen needed someone to be there for him, someone to love and care for him no matter what.

And I... I did. It was too early to admit it out loud, but I was so sure I already did.

I was just happy being around him. I wasn't sure if it was something about me or my medication. Most blokes my age were crazy about sex, constantly horny. At least according to conversations I picked up at school and what was portrayed on television.

I wasn't like that, though.

It must be my medication; it could affect the sex drive. It was something I should take up with my doctor, but as I wasn't about to have sex in the near future, there really wasn't much point.

Maybe I would later, when Jørgen and I had progressed further. Maybe, if I brought it up to my doctor, we'd have to change dosage or my whole medication and I would be even more suspect to seizures until things smoothed out.

As it was now, I tended to have seizures a couple of times a month. That wasn't much, compared to how it had been before. I had them a lot more often in primary school.

My medication worked better now, so once or twice a month was a good thing. I knew some could live without seizures for years, but I didn't dare hope that would ever be the case for me.

That was just setting myself up for disappointment. I had it good now, I couldn't complain.

The vegetable package started dripping.

"Ah, shit—" I jerked it away from my face so it would stop dripping on my jogging bottoms and went downstairs to put it back in the freezer. I took out another package of peas and laid it gingerly over the side of my face.

"Hey, Geir—"

Dad came wandering into the kitchen, but he stopped once he got a look at me. "What happened to you?" He grabbed my arm and forced it away from my face. He inspected the damage, then shook his head. "Who did this?"

"Just some bloke at school." I went over to sit down on a kitchen chair. I could tell Dad wasn't about to let this go. He sat down too, beside me. "It was my own fault, really. If I hadn't spoken back to him he would've let me be."

"What did he do to you to even make you have to talk back to him?"

"Nothing much. He was just spouting off some nasty things, and he tried to trip me. Really, Dad, it's not a big deal."

"What kinds of nasty things does he say?" Dad took a gentle hold of my chin and he turned my face back around so he could look at my eye again. "He must've hit you hard to give you that shiner, son. Is this something that happens often?"

"He's never hit me before, no." It was the first time Jonas had physically hit me. Usually he was happy with just tripping me or shoving me into things.

"What does he say to you, then?" Dad let my chin go, and I put the pea package back to cool it down.

"Just things." This wasn't the way I wanted to have this conversation with my dad.

"What kinds of things?"

"Lately he's been very keen on poof, fag, fairy, queer. All of that." Ever since he saw my sketchbook, it had all been about my sexuality. Nothing more about my epilepsy or my general looks, just homophobic comments.

Dad was silent for a while, but his eyes were trained on me. "Are you gay?" His voice was decidedly neutral. His face was expressionless too.

"Yeah." I swallowed. "I wanted to talk to you about that."

"About being gay?" He was still expressionless.

"Well, yeah. But also about, uh… Well, there's *someone*. I wanted to ask you about Easter. I want to invite him to the cabin with us." I'd been thinking about it for a while now.

We were going away to my uncle and aunt's cabin for the entire Easter holiday, and I didn't want to leave Jørgen. I wanted to be with him, and I could only imagine he needed to get away for a bit too, so… inviting him had seemed like a good idea. If only my dad would agree to it.

Dad frowned now and my stomach plummeted. "Is this someone you've met at school?"

"Uh, no. He's a bit older than me, but we're taking things slow."

"How much older is a bit older?" His frown deepened.

My chest felt hollow.

This wasn't going to go well.

"He's twenty-two. There's nothing wrong with that, Dad. Even if we had been doing anything, which we're not, it wouldn't be illegal. I'm perfectly legal. Besides, as I said, we're taking things slow. I just thought it would be nice to have him join me at the cabin. Marika's bringing her boyfriend."

"So he's your boyfriend?"

"Well, no, not really. We haven't talked about that. We just like to spend time together. There's more there, but we're taking things slow. Very slow."

He dragged a hand over his face. "Look, Geir—"

"Dad! We're not doing anything wrong. He's a really nice person, you know. If you're thinking he's taking advantage of me or whatever, I can assure you he's not! He's the one who wanted us to take it slow in the first place—"

"Geir, please!" Dad held up his hands. "I've been meaning to talk to you since I got home. I had planned on sitting down with you last night, but we were having such a good time. So I'm going to tell you now." He leaned an elbow on the table. "Charlotte and I have decided to move in together."

I blinked.

"We have decided to move in together in her house, in Oslo."

It was like those words echoed around the kitchen.

"I know you haven't applied for your third year at school yet. The deadline's a month away, but if you want to continue school, there are many good ones down in Oslo you can apply to. Better than the one here."

"Dad—no, Dad. We can't *move!*"

"You haven't got any friends here. Did you think I hadn't noticed? I thought you'd be happy to be able to move away, to start over somewhere new."

"I've got Jørgen." Something good had finally happened in my life and now my dad wanted to drag me away from it. It wasn't fair—it wasn't fair *at all*.

"A man who's too old for you."

"He's *not!*" I stood up, anger surging through me. How could Dad do this to me? "He's the best thing to ever happen to me, Dad. He likes me for who I am. No one else around here has ever done that! I'm the freak who's got epilepsy. No one wants anything to do with me, but Jørgen does! You can't make me leave!"

Dad stood up as well, and I could tell he was angry too. "You might be old enough to manage your sex life, Geir, but you're still only seventeen and I'm your father. That means I decide where you'll be living until you're eighteen, and you'll be coming with me to Oslo!"

"You can't make me!" I could feel my eyes burn. I didn't want to cry in front of him. I hadn't cried in front of Dad in years.

"I bloody well can! We're moving to Oslo once you finish school this summer, and that's the end of the discussion!"

I turned on my heel and left. I couldn't look at him, couldn't say another word to him without breaking down. My jacket was pulled on in jerky movements and I managed to lace up my boots despite my shaking hands.

The door slammed shut as I left.

I regretted not bringing Charo once I was out on the street, but going back in for him would have defeated the whole purpose.

There was only one place I wanted to go. I'd forgotten both scarf and gloves, so I huddled in my jacket all the way towards Jørgen's flat while fighting tears.

I rang Jørgen's doorbell with shaking fingers.

How was I supposed to tell him there was suddenly an expiration date on our tentative relationship? That my own dad was forcing me to leave town?

I didn't even know what Jørgen had gone through yet—all I knew was that it must've been terrible for him. I could guess, but something told me there was more to it, I just didn't know what.

The door opened and I lifted my head.

It wasn't Jørgen standing there. This bloke was Jørgen's height, but all resemblance ended there. He had dark auburn hair, freckles, brown eyes, and a wide smile. He was good-looking, but he had nothing on Jørgen.

"Can I help you?" he asked as he eyed me up and down.

"Is Jørgen here?" I wrapped my arms around myself and dropped my head. My eyes burned again from fighting tears. I didn't want to cry in front of this stranger.

"Yeah, just a sec." He took a step back and turned around. "Hey, Jørgen! Some cute bloke's here to see you!"

I blushed.

Jørgen appeared over the man's shoulder. I'd seen Jørgen in a tee before, but a tee covered up a heck of a lot. Jørgen was only wearing a vest now, leaving his upper arms and a lot of his shoulders bare, and a black, intricate tribal tattoo was inked into his skin on both shoulders.

Jørgen's friend started laughing, and my gaze jerked over to him in surprise. He wasn't looking at me, however, but back at Jørgen. "You got him mesmerised, all right, mate."

Jørgen stared at him, unimpressed. "Go away."

His friend only laughed again and motioned to me.

"I need to talk to you." I was surprised my voice was even steady, considering my roiling emotions and the fact that Jørgen had left me completely, well, *mesmerised*, to use the other bloke's words, by that tattoo.

Jørgen nodded. "Tarjei was just leaving."

"I was not."

"Get out." Jørgen levelled another stare at him.

Tarjei heaved a sigh, but he did start to pull his jacket on. "Yeah, yeah. I can tell *someone* wants privacy." He waggled his eyebrows suggestively.

Jørgen's eyes narrowed. "Get. Out."

Jørgen motioned for me to come in, and I brushed past him as I scrambled inside. He reached out to settle a hand on my back, and I caught Tarjei's gaze zooming in on that movement.

He looked at Jørgen almost in wonder, but Jørgen's focus was on me now.

"Are you all right?"

I shook my head slightly. Being close to Jørgen made me feel better, but the thought that I wouldn't be able to be close to him soon had my stomach plummeting.

Tarjei stepped outside. He cast one last lingering gaze at me, then turned to Jørgen. "Ring me later." And with that, he shut the door.

Jørgen's eyes narrowed further as he continued to look down at me. "What happened to your face? Who did that to you?"

"Happened at school. It was Jonas. I talked back and he hit me." I gingerly touched my cheekbone. I knew it bruised, both it and the corner of my eye. I probably looked worse than I had when I'd got home from school. "That's not why I'm here, though." The tears pressed again, burning my eyes.

Jørgen seemed worried. "Come in. We can sit down."

I hung up my jacket and put my boots away, then followed him into the living room. Jørgen sat down on the sofa, directly opposite the telly, while I curled up in the corner.

I wrapped my around my folded knees. "Dad is forcing me to move to Oslo with him once school lets out," I said into my kneecaps. "He's not giving me a choice."

I slowly lifted my head to gauge Jørgen's reaction. He stared straight ahead at the telly, which was on mute.

"Why Oslo?" Jørgen asked eventually.

"His girlfriend. They want to move in together." I pressed the palm of my hands to my eyes, wincing as it pressed against the bruised and tender skin on my right side. "I don't want to l-leave." And just like that the tears fell. I couldn't keep them at bay anymore.

"Hey…"

Jørgen scooted close to me. He reached out, but his hand hovered above mine for a bit. He eventually settled it on my shoulder, and I took that as invitation to lean in closer to him.

When he didn't react, I rested my head against his collarbone and slid my arms around his torso.

He was more hesitant, but he did wrap his arms around me, and that was more than enough comfort for me.

"How can he do this to me? I've lived here my whole life, and now he's just expecting me to pack up and go willingly? I don't want to leave." I sobbed now, and tears still ran from my eyes.

They were wetting his vest and skin, and it

couldn't be comfortable for him, but he didn't say anything about it. He just held me tight.

"Maybe..." He trailed off and swallowed, then cleared his voice. "Maybe it'll be good for you."

"What?" I stiffened.

"I mean—Getting away from here, starting over. Maybe it'll be good. Maybe you'll start to enjoy school, have proper friends. You won't be alone when your dad's at work. You'll have someone else there to be around you, besides Charo."

I pulled away and wiped furiously at my cheeks. "Why are saying all of that? Do you want me to leave?"

"I don't want you to go. Of course I don't." He rubbed my back softly. "But he's your dad, and until you're eighteen you have to go with what he decides. You're not legal."

"It's just a year. A year until I'm eighteen, and *now* he decided that we're moving. He could've decided that ages ago, not *now* when I've met you and things are going great. If he wants to move, he could've waited a bloody *year*, so he wouldn't have to drag me with him. I don't want to go!" I broke down in sobs again. I leaned back into his arms and he held me close as I cried. "It's so unfair!"

"That's life." It wasn't the answer I'd hoped for, but that was Jørgen, wasn't it?

179

He was reserved, troubled. He'd experienced a lot worse things in life than I ever had. I was either ignored or bullied in school, and now my dad wanted me to move to Oslo.

Jørgen hadn't told me what had happened to him, but it was so much worse than the sorry excuse I had for a life.

"I don't want to go home tonight," I blurted out.

Silence. Long silence.

"You can stay here."

"Really?" I sniffled. "You wouldn't mind?"

Another moment's silence.

"No, I won't." He ran a hand over my cheek, wiping away my tears.

I sniffled again, but the tears were starting to dry up now. I'd stay over at Jørgen's flat. In Jørgen's *bed*. I hadn't been in his bed since our first meeting, and then I hadn't even been aware of it until I woke up in a strange place, disoriented.

I was going to spend the *night* with him.

CHAPTER 15

I woke up to an empty bed.

I stretched, then felt the other side. It was cold. I had no idea what time it was, but I knew it was the middle of the night, because it was dark outside. I didn't feel rested at all, and Jørgen certainly couldn't have slept much if the other side of the bed was cold.

He'd gone to bed with me, but I had no idea how long he'd stayed, as I'd fallen asleep immediately.

I threw the duvet off and stood up. I'd slept in my jogging bottoms and T-shirt.

Nothing had happened between us, besides him holding me as I cried.

He wasn't ready for anything. I wasn't ready

either, but it was fine. We had something nice going on and it was wonderful the way it was.

Jørgen was in the living room. He was lying on his back on the sofa, and for a moment I thought he was asleep.

The next moment, I was afraid he was in the middle of another flashback. I went through everything I'd read online—but then he turned his head to look at me.

"Why aren't you in bed?" I asked quietly, walking over to him. The sofa was wide, so I perched at the edge, right next to his hips.

"I can't sleep," he replied, just as quietly.

"Why not? Is it because of me?" I twisted my hands together in my lap.

"Yeah, but not like you think." He met my gaze. "I can't sleep if there's someone else in the room with me. Or I can fall asleep, but the single tiniest movement wake me up, and it's just not worth it. The little sleep I can get is not worth it when I wake up terrified by a small movement."

"Why are you so terrified?" I put a hand tentatively on his chest. "What's happened to you to make you not able to sleep properly?"

He was serious when he looked at me. "You don't want to know. Trust me. You're better off not knowing."

I bit my lower lip. God, it must have been something really horrible. "Can you sleep on the sofa?"

"Not really, no. It's too hard." He laughed humourlessly and ran both hands over his face.

"Then come to bed." I splayed my hand out on his chest, but otherwise I didn't move. "It's your bed. You shouldn't have to leave it just because of me. Do you want me to go home?" If he said so, I would leave. I wanted him to sleep, I didn't want him to stay awake so *I* could sleep.

He stared at me for long, silent moments. "I won't be able to sleep."

"Just try. I'm going to be as still as I possibly can." I stood up and held my hand out to him. He stared at that too, and I was starting to fear he wouldn't take it when he finally did.

We walked back into the bedroom and got in on our respective sides.

I started out on my back, but I didn't like sleeping on my back, so I turned on my side. I turned on the side away from him, in case that made it easier for him. I didn't know what would trigger him, besides crowds. I didn't know how to make him feel better either, and it honestly sucked.

He made me feel good, and all I wanted was to make *him* feel good.

I rolled over until I faced him.

He was on his back, staring up at the ceiling.

"If I do anything that's uncomfortable for you... You'll tell me, right?"

He tilted his head towards me. "Trust me, even if I don't say anything, you'll notice it."

That wasn't exactly what I'd wanted to hear.

"Do you still want us to be— I mean— uh, do you want us to— Even though I have to leave in a couple of months?"

"I do like you." He turned his head so he wasn't facing me anymore. It was dark in the room, but I could still see his profile. "I never thought I ever could be close to anyone, but you've proven I can in such a short time. I—I don't want to *not* see you anymore."

Well, that was a confession if I'd ever heard one. "Then can we just—I don't know, like, continue this? I don't want to stop seeing you. You've made me feel better about myself. I don't want to lose you."

"I'm not going anywhere," he murmured.

I flopped on my back again.

"I wish I was eighteen." I sighed. I was all cried out, but I had a funny feeling in my chest.

"Yeah." He sighed too.

Silence fell over us then.

My mind went to Dad and the impending move.

What was I supposed to do in Oslo? How could I

be safe there? Oslo was a big city, for Norway, anyway, and if Dad's girlfriend didn't live right smack in the middle of central Oslo, everything would be very far to travel to and from.

What if I had a seizure on a train or a bus or a tram? What if I had a seizure out on the street? My impression of Oslo wasn't that people tended to care for or help each other much.

Even in this small town people weren't exactly willing to approach me if I had a seizure. It looked scary and freaky. In Oslo, people would probably assume I was a drug addict.

"A year's not that long, you know," Jørgen said. "It goes by in a flash. When the year's done, you'll be eighteen. You can do whatever you want."

"I want to come back."

I hadn't even left yet and it was all I could think about. And it wasn't just because of Jørgen either. Aside from the hell I suffered at school, I actually liked the town. I liked walking Charo on the hiking trails, alone or with Jørgen, it didn't matter.

I liked that it was a small town, with not the greatest choice in shops, and that if we ever needed anything bigger we could just drive a town or two over and there'd be more to choose from.

"You might not want that next year, after experiencing big city life."

"Oh, I will. I've been to Oslo. There's nothing special about it." It'd been a couple of years since I'd been there, but I remembered it well. It was too big for me. Dad had said so too, but I guess after meeting Charlotte he'd changed his mind.

For a second I wished he'd never met her, but then I felt bad. Dad had been alone ever since Mum died. He deserved to be happy again.

I just wished his happiness wouldn't mean the end of mine.

"Do you mind if I turn on the lamp?"

"What? No." I turned to him in surprise. "Aren't you tired?"

"I am, but I'd prefer to keep it on. If you don't mind?"

I shook my head. It was a bit awkward as I was lying down, but I managed it to a certain extent.

He leaned over and turned the lamp on, and for a brief moment I got a good look at his shoulder and the back of his neck. The tribal tattoo stretched out over both shoulder blades, over his shoulders, and partway down his upper arms. I wondered how far down his back it went...

"When'd you get that tattoo done?"

He flopped down on his back again and glanced briefly at me. "A few years ago."

"Does it have a special meaning to you?"

I could see him stiffen next to me, and I instantly regretted the question. It was a normal question, wasn't it? It's what people would ask if they spotted someone who had a tattoo.

"Not a particular meaning, no. It was more like— well, I wanted to cover up scars. It doesn't do the best job, but I think the scars are a little less obvious now."

I couldn't help but look over at him again at that. "You have a lot of scars, haven't you?"

"Yeah."

I closed my eyes. I wished I knew what he'd gone through, but at the same time I wasn't sure I wanted to know. It was horrible, and I didn't want to hear it. But if I knew, I might be able to avoid triggering subjects.

"Stop thinking," Jørgen told me quietly. "Go to sleep."

I rolled over with my back to him, my eyes still closed. "Good night, Jørgen." I could respect that he didn't want to talk anymore. It was a sore subject, and I wasn't going to push him.

"Good night."

I thought I was going to have a hard time falling asleep again, what with everything, but I soon nodded off.

I didn't know how long I slept for, because I was

startled awake by a thrashing body next to me.

Disoriented, I pushed up on my elbows and turned my head.

Jørgen's eyes were closed, he was asleep, but he must be having quite a nightmare, because he still thrashed around.

I pushed myself up in a sitting position and reached over to touch him.

Jørgen sat up so abruptly I shrank back in surprise. Beads of sweat were gathered on his forehead and his pale blue eyes were wide. His breathing was erratic too, and just like that I realised what I'd done.

I'd touched him, without him being aware of me touching him.

"Oh, Jørgen, I'm so sorry!" I clapped my hands to my mouth as he curled in on himself, hands tangling in his hair and pulling.

"No, no, no, no," he muttered, not even reacting to my voice.

"Can you hear me? Jørgen?" I scooted closer, but not too close. If he reacted to something, if he thought I was someone else, he might actually lash out. I wasn't strong enough to fight off a full-grown, fit man. "Jørgen? Jørgen, it's me. Geir. We're in your bedroom. It's still night out, but it's light in the room because you wanted the lamp on. Jørgen?

Would you look at me, please? I'm not going to hurt you."

He didn't react at first, so I kept rambling about the interior of the room and the sheets being tangled up around him.

Eventually, his erratic breathing slowed down, and soon his fingers released the clutching hold on his hair.

He lifted his head.

"Jørgen?" I asked again, unsure if he was back or if he was still trapped in a flashback. "Jørgen?"

He swallowed, ran his hands over his face, then fell back on the bed. "I'm so sorry."

I scooted over to his side. "Don't be. Don't be sorry. You can't help it."

"These are my issues. You shouldn't have to deal with them." He didn't remove his hands from his eyes.

"I wasn't lying when I said I don't mind." My voice rose a bit without me meaning it to, but hopefully Jørgen got the memo. "I'm here for you, whatever it is. If I can be of even a little help, I'll be happy. Now that I know what I'm dealing with, it's a lot easier for me to, well, deal with."

He didn't answer, just shook his head.

I wasn't sure if it was for me, or for him, so I didn't comment on it.

"Can I touch you?"

A barely there shake of his head.

I lay back down on the bed as well, but kept myself at a distance to him. If he didn't want me close, I had to respect that.

"Did this happen because of me?" I asked in a low voice. "You said the tiniest movement could cause you to wake up in a panic. Did I cause this?"

"I don't know. I have no idea. It happens when I'm alone too, so maybe not."

I flicked my tongue out to wet my lips. "Maybe if I keep staying over, you'll get used to me." I said it lightly, teasingly.

Deep down I really hoped it would be true.

He sounded lighter as well when he replied. "Yeah, maybe I will."

CHAPTER 16

"**S**ure you don't want me to drop you off at school too?" Jørgen looked at me from the driver's side of the car.

I shook my head.

"I'm skipping today. I'm not in the mood to deal with Jonas atop it all. But thanks for the offer." I managed a small smile. "Are we walking Charo later today?"

"If you want." He still had one hand gripping the steering wheel, even if we were parked outside my home. The other rested on his thigh.

I reached out to touch it softly, running my fingers over his knuckles. His hand twitched a bit but stayed where it was.

"I do. I'm looking forward to it already."

He stared down at our hands, then glanced up at me. "I'll see you after work, then."

I nodded again. "Yeah. See you." I got out of the car and waved at him through the window after closing the door behind me.

He waved back, then shifted the car into gear.

I watched as he drove off down the road, not towards his flat, but towards his workplace. I'd see him again in a little over eight hours. I couldn't wait.

Dad was there the moment I stepped through the door, looking both angry and worried at the same time. "Where have you been? I've been ringing you non-stop!"

"Can you blame me?" I snapped, anger surging up again now that I was back home and facing him. "You're forcing me to move away!"

"I'm doing this for our own good."

"Your own good, maybe. Not mine." I stalked up the stairs.

"You've got school!"

"I am not going!" I slammed my bedroom door.

I dropped down on my bed and lay staring at the ceiling, a lot like I'd done last night.

After falling asleep again, we'd slept through the rest of the night. Jørgen hadn't had another night-mare, not that I'd been able to tell.

It was difficult for me to gauge his moods since he was so stoic most of the time, but I was pretty sure he'd been in a good mood this morning.

I must've dozed off, because next I knew Dad was in my room.

I blinked myself awake and rubbed my eyes. Then used my arms to push myself up in a sitting position.

"You haven't taken your medication today." Dad held out a plate with two pieces of toast and my pills next to them. He put a glass of orange juice on my bedside table.

I took a tentative bite of the toast. It was still warm.

"Geir, we need to talk." Dad ran a hand through his hair and sighed. He sat down on the edge of my bed. "I'm sorry I yelled at you. I shouldn't have done that. But I honestly thought you'd be happy about moving, considering what life's like for you here. When you weren't… I was hurt, because I thought this would be something we would both be excited about, something we would both embrace as a new adventure."

"I'm sorry I yelled at you, too," I mumbled around another piece of toast.

"I know you haven't even met Charlotte, and I should've considered that. Of course you wouldn't like moving so far away without even having met the woman I'm moving in with. I should've thought about that, but I was so excited that we're taking our relationship to the next level. I'm sorry for not considering you in all of that." Dad looked at me. "You're not angry at me because you think I'm replacing Mum, are you? Because I'm not. No one could ever replace your mum."

"I don't think that. I'm happy that you've found someone. Really, I am."

Dad smiled in relief. "I'm glad to hear that. Charlotte is very special to me. But you don't know her, and you should, so I have invited her to come up here for Easter. Her children will spend Easter with their dad, but Charlotte will be here to spend it with us."

"She's coming here or are we still going to the cabin?"

I was slowly losing my appetite. Dad had invited his girlfriend, yet he wasn't acknowledging the fact that I had someone I wanted to invite as well. I put the plate beside the glass of orange juice on my bedside table.

"The cabin, yes. It'll be the first time Daniel and Carina meet her too. Marika, as well, and now we'll finally get to meet her boyfriend." Dad's eyes fell to my plate and he frowned, then pressed his lips tightly together. "So you— you spent the night at your boyfriend's place?"

"Yeah." I didn't bother pointing out that we weren't exactly *boyfriends*. Heading that way, maybe, but a proper relationship was a long way off.

"You said he was twenty-two." Dad wasn't looking at me now. He staredat his own lap. "Don't you think that that's a bit old for you? You've just turned seventeen."

"If I'd been in my twenties, this wouldn't even be an issue. It's only because I haven't passed the big twenty yet, it suddenly seems like such a big age difference. But it's really not." I leant back against the headboard. "I think it's really unfair of you to judge my relationship. You don't know what kind of rela- tionship we have, so you have no right to have an opinion about it. Jørgen is a really nice bloke and he's done nothing but be kind to me."

"I can see that, but you have to understand I am worried. He is a lot older than you, and he's your first boyfriend. I don't like the thought of him being so much older than you, with you being so inexpe- rienced."

"He would never force me to do anything! We're taking things slow, Dad. Very, *very* slow. Do you have a problem with me being gay? Because it sounds like it. You say it's about him, but we've done nothing wrong."

"I don't have a problem with that. I am surprised, though, because you've never even hinted about it."

"It wasn't relevant before."

"Is it something you do often, sleep over at his place?" Dad swiftly changed the subject.

"No," I muttered. "This was only the second time. The first time I didn't even know I was spending the night, because the seizure knocked me out. He took me in, without even knowing who I was, so I could rest. He's the kindest person I know, and all he wants is for me to be happy." I fingered the yin-yang ornament around my neck.

It was one of my most prized possessions—I only took it off when I showered.

"That was nice of him."

"Yeah, it was. That's who he is. A good person." I took another piece of toast. "I think you should meet him. At least let me invite him to the cabin this Easter. You're bringing your girlfriend, Marika's bringing her boyfriend. I'm going to be left out, and if you're forcing me to move with you, I want to spend the rest of the time I've got left with him."

Dad sighed heavily.

"You're not going to stop me from seeing him."

"I don't want to stop you. I am just voicing my concern about your age difference. I remember what it was like to be your age, and *his* age. He might expect certain things that you're not ready to give—or things that you can't give."

"Oh God." I groaned and tilted my head back. "Don't give me a sex talk. It would only embarrass the both of us. Besides, we're not even at that point. *He* wants us to go slow, because he's not ready. And I'm fine with that, because I'm not ready either."

"He's not ready?" Dad perked up a bit. "Why, though? Why does *he* want to wait?"

"I can't tell you that, because I don't know myself. I suspect, and some of my suspicions have been kind of confirmed. He's had a hard life. When I kissed him, it was his *first* kiss." That was probably a bit too TMI for my dad, but he needed to understand. He needed to know that Jørgen would never force me into anything, not after what he'd been through.

Dad's eyes flicked from me to the floor, back to me again, and finally settled on the plate and glass of orange juice. "Please take your medication, Geir. You're already late."

I took the pills grudgingly and swallowed them with the orange juice. They didn't taste any good, but the orange juice masked it well. After swallowing, I took another piece of toast.

"Maybe, when Charlotte gets here..." Dad shook his head. "Maybe we could meet, all four of us? Have lunch or dinner, perhaps?"

I blinked in surprise.

"Y-yeah. That would be awesome." I wasn't about to question it, because I didn't want him to change his mind again.

Now my only worry was if Jørgen would actually agree to meet my dad.

I DIDN'T BRING up the subject until Jørgen and I were well on our way up a pretty simple hiking trail we'd taken many times. It wasn't the most accessible trail, thus it wasn't very popular, and we were a lot more likely to be left alone than if we took any of the others.

Charo was, as per usual, without a leash, and he walked ahead of us both. Jørgen was ahead of me too on the steep, narrow trail.

"So Dad wants to meet you."

Jørgen stopped dead in his tracks and I almost walked right into him.

"He what?" He turned around to stare down at me.

"He wants to meet you. I'm supposed to meet Charlotte, his girlfriend, and I pointed out how hypocritical he was being. So now he wants to meet you."

"Hypocritical?" Jørgen raised an eyebrow.

"Yeah. I mean, he had some issues with our age difference. I pointed out some things to him, and now he seems okay with it. It's only five years. It's not much."

"Six years. My birthday's in August, so... six years."

"It's still not much." I didn't know if he'd been arguing or just stating facts, but still. "Just as I told Dad, if I'd been in my twenties as well, a meagre age difference of six years would be nothing."

"That's true," he said with a small nod. "I've thought about our age difference, though. You're young, you've got so much ahead of you. I've been thinking, in terms of being saddled with someone like me."

"What's that supposed to mean?" I tilted my head, indignant. "I think you're wonderful."

He shook his head, then started back up the slope. "I've got some major issues that you shouldn't have to deal with when you're so young."

"You're being awfully negative all of a sudden."

I hurried to keep up with him. He was taller than me, had longer legs, so he easily strode up the steep trail, whereas as I had to scramble around for something to hold onto to get myself up.

It would be a lot easier in the summer, when we weren't walking on slippery, packed snow.

Then again, when summer came around, I had to move away from all this.

"It's the truth."

"Well, I don't care."

Jørgen chuckled.

"What?" I stared at his back. "What's so funny?"

"You are. When you say stuff like that, you do sound your age."

Jørgen had reached the top of the steep trail, and I pushed myself up the last part by holding onto the trunk of a small, askew tree sticking out of the earth.

"I don't mean that in a bad way, because you *are* only seventeen, and that's how you *should* act."

I stared up at him. "That sounds an awful lot like you're saying I'm a twat."

"I'm not." Jørgen's arms were suddenly around my waist, and he drew me in close to him. I went willingly. "I was just pointing it out. You usually seem older than you are, maybe not in looks, but in personality."

"Yeah, well. Maybe I feel older." I slid my arms around his torso. It was a bit awkward with both our thick winter jackets in the way, but it was manageable. "I certainly don't have much in common with other seventeen-year-olds." I didn't have *anything* in common with people my age. Not anyone I'd ever met, anyway.

Jørgen didn't reply, just held me tight for a couple of minutes.

I didn't complain, just enjoyed feeling him close to me even if we were both donned up in winter gear. I only closed my eyes and buried my face against his neck. Well, his scarf, anyway.

In such a short time, I'd fallen head over heels for him.

And soon I'd have to leave him.

I wanted to pursue this between us, see where it was going, but Dad wasn't giving me that chance. I understood Dad, I did—he just wanted to be happy. He'd found someone to be happy with, and that was awesome.

But I wanted to be happy too, and I knew I could be happy with Jørgen.

He already made me feel so good.

"Do you really want me to meet your dad?"

I'd almost forgotten what had started this whole conversation. "Yeah, I guess. He's sceptical and I want him to see that there's nothing to worry about. I think he thinks that you're some sort of predator. I tried to convince him you're not, but he's pretty set on the whole age difference issue."

Jørgen stiffened against me, and I realised too late what I'd just said.

I held my breath, hoping it wouldn't set a flash-back or a panic attack in motion, but Jørgen slowly relaxed again when I didn't continue to speak.

Note to self, don't make references to sexual predators or abusers.

When I finally drew back to look at him, his gaze fell on me. His eyes were darker than normal, and his expression serious.

"I would never force you into anything," he said, voice low and intense. "Never."

"I know." I cupped his cheek in my gloved hand and stepped in close again. "I *know*. That's what I want Dad to see too, so maybe he wouldn't be so against me spending time with you."

Jørgen pressed his lips tighter together. "If it means something to you, I'll—I'll meet him."

"I appreciate that. Thank you."

I leaned up and kissed him softly. He responded quicker this time, but it wasn't as frantic as it had been the last time. It was a gentle kiss, only lips sliding against lips.

It was good, oh so good, and both relaxing and slightly arousing.

I hoped our future would be full of kisses like these.

If we even had a future.

PART V
WATCH AS MY WORLD ENDS

JØRGEN

CHAPTER 17

"This is where we're meeting?"

I looked up at the sign of the building housing the Brasserie. I was tensing up rapidly, and my anxiety reared its ugly head.

Of course this was where we were headed. I was very aware of that. I just didn't want to be there.

"What's wrong?" Geir looked up at the sign too. It was a nice sign. The Brasserie was our town's finest place to go for lunch or dinners, though dinners were a lot more expensive than their lunch menu.

"My brother works here."

"Oh."

I could tell Geir was baffled; he didn't seem to know what to say to that. I hadn't expected anything more. He'd seen me suffer both a flashback and a panic attack the last time I'd been faced with my brother. It couldn't have been a pretty sight for him.

"Jo's more a barman than a waiter, though, so he usually works nights."

"Then he's most likely not here," Geir said optimistically.

"Yeah…" With my bad luck, he probably would be there. If life found a way to fuck with me, it did.

Things had been going pretty well for a couple of months now, but his move to Oslo came nearer and nearer, while I fell deeper and deeper—in love, that was, not the usual depression.

The depression would come, though, tenfold, the moment Geir left.

I knew it would, because I bloody *cared* about him, and it wasn't going away either. I hated thinking about the beginning of summer, because that was when school let out, and that again led to Geir being gone. I couldn't bear to think about it.

"Dad chose the place. He wanted to take Charlotte out to a fancy lunch after he picked her up at the airport. He extended the invitation to us, which was really nice of him. I'd expected he wanted to stay alone with her."

"He wants you to meet her," I said. "You're the most important person in his life and he wants you to meet his new, second most important person."

Thinking about that kept my anxiety in check. Geir's dad wanted Geir to meet his new *girlfriend*.

That's what I focused on, not the fact that he also wanted to meet me. Being anxious about this meeting was something I could deal with, but coupled with the anxiety of meeting Geir's dad in my brother's workplace had me on the verge of losing it.

And I couldn't let that happen.

Geir wanted me to meet his dad, to prove I wasn't some kind of monster taking advantage of his son. I needed to be myself, without the anxiety rippling through me. Having an anxiety attack would be bearable, but if it progressed into a flashback or a panic attack, it would be *bad*.

Not only would every guest in there see what a lunatic I was, but Geir's dad would, and it would certainly not endear me to him at all.

I had to pull myself together, but it was hard. I'd lived with my issues for most of my life, they were a part of me, and I couldn't shut them off no matter how much I wanted to.

I glanced at Geir, taking in the slight smile on his lips as he looked around the outside tables of the Brasserie. He'd just been a kid I'd taken in to help him, but then he'd turned into so much more.

He'd wormed his way into my life, under my skin, and he'd stuck there. It wasn't something I could be bitter or angry about, because he was wonderful. I had him in my life, for the time being, and it made things a tiny bit better.

"Are you ready to go in?" Geir asked softly.

"Yeah." I wasn't ready at all, but we couldn't stand outside for much longer. We already looked weird, lingering in front of the building instead of going in.

Geir smiled at me in encouragement. He walked ahead of me, but I made sure to hold the door open for him as he went inside. He gave me another smile at that before heading into the restaurant.

The moment couldn't be delayed anymore.

His dad rose from a table that sat four, and a blonde, slim woman rose at his side.

Geir smiled at his dad and greeted Charlotte warmly. What they said went straight by me.

I was going to have to greet Geir's dad, who already didn't like me because I was older than his son. How could he even begin to like me if he found out just how messed up I was? How could I convince him I was a normal, functioning human being when just being inside the restaurant made my skin crawl and my breath quicken?

"Dad, this is Jørgen." Geir turned to me. "Jørgen, this is my Dad."

I took two steps forward to bring me close

enough to shake his hand. My hand was clammy. I wish I'd wiped it on my jeans, but it was too late now. His hand was dry and firm.

"Jørgen Lister. Nice to meet you."

"Yngvar Berger." He nodded. It wasn't much but at least it was something.

"Hi. I'm Charlotte Bergman." His girlfriend seemed a lot nicer and accommodating.

We sat down. Geir thankfully sat across from his dad, leaving me the spot opposite Charlotte.

It would be a lot better to sit opposite her welcoming smile. I couldn't tell what Yngvar thought and it made me antsy and uncomfortable.

Geir handed me the menu.

"Aren't you going to look at it?" I asked in a low voice.

"I know what I'm having. What I'm always having when Dad and I do lunch here." He grinned.

I'd never eaten lunch here before. I'd never been inside, period. Jo worked here, and I couldn't stand being around so many people, least of all him.

I scanned the menu, settling on something easy.

I ended up next to Geir's dad when we went up to the bar counter. He and Charlotte ordered first, then they turned to me next.

So did the bloke behind the bar, and his eyes

widened slightly as he looked at me. Dread crept down my spine.

"You must be Jo's brother!" He beamed at me. "You look so alike, it's like you could be twins."

My hand, resting atop the bar, started to shake. I didn't want to hear talk about Jo, especially not how I looked like him.

If we were so alike, why had our uncle singled me out? What was so appealing about me, but not him? Why had Jo got away untouched? Why was he so much better than me?

Geir's hand squeezed mine tightly, almost to the point of pain, and I held on to him.

"I'd like the chicken bruschetta," Geir said, neatly cutting off any further conversation between myself and the bloke. "Actually, make that two."

It wasn't what I'd decided on, but I didn't mind. I liked chicken, I liked bread, and I liked salad. As long as I didn't have to talk to that bloke, I'd be happy.

Why did he have to bring up Jo? And in front of Geir's dad...

He was going to think I was mental. I *was* mental, but he wouldn't have known that if it hadn't been for this nosy twat.

Yngvar had paid for all four of our meals before I managed to bring myself back enough for actual conversation. I hadn't wanted him to pay for me, I could very well pay my own, but it was already done and there was no use arguing the point now.

Geir tugged my hand, which he still held. "Come on, let's go back to the table."

"Thank you." I squeezed his hand again and rubbed my thumb over the back of it.

"I'm glad I could be of help."

We sat down at our places at the table.

I could feel Yngvar's eyes on me. I didn't dare look up to meet them, though.

"So you have a brother?"

"Dad—"

"Yeah. I do." I nodded slightly. "Older brother. He works here." I was so very, very grateful that Jo wasn't working now. I couldn't have even sat at this table with him nearby.

There had been many a night I'd been in bed, crying, or locked in the basement, crying, wishing that for once I could be spared and Jo could take my place. It was a horrible thought, but after everything... I'd just wanted to not be hurt anymore.

Why had my uncle desired me so much, but not cared about Jo, even though we looked almost identical? Why had Mum hated me while she'd been perfectly civil to Jo? Every single one of them had liked Jo, while me...

I hadn't been worth a thing. I was just someone

she could vent her anger on, someone she could punish and lock in the basement or in a closet or—

I shook my head and pressed my hands against my eyes. I couldn't think about it. I'd suffer a flashback for sure then, and I could darn well pay money on that a panic attack would follow.

"I have to go to the toilet."

I pushed away from the table and strode through the restaurant to the toilets. They were blessedly empty, and I leaned back against the door for several seconds before I went over to the sink. I stared at myself in the mirror and found I looked normal enough.

I splashed some cold water in my face and neck, then dabbed it off with a few wads of paper. When I was dry again, I took many deep breaths. I didn't calm down completely, but I reckoned it was enough.

I walked back out into the restaurant.

I spotted Geir leaning forward on his elbows, staring intently at his dad. As I got closer, I caught what he was saying.

"Stop pushing him, Dad. He doesn't like talking about his brother. They don't have a good relationship, so just let it lie. In fact, let everything family related lie."

"How am I supposed to get to know him then, if I

can't ask about his family?" Yngvar hissed back. "It's a standard topic of conversation."

"Think of something else!"

Charlotte spotted me, and her eyes went slightly wider than normal for a moment before she smiled welcomingly.

I managed to return it, barely.

Yngvar caught sight of me too then, and when Geir noticed that his attention was diverted, he turned to me. He sat back in his chair and smiled as well.

I slid back down on my chair. "I'm sorry," I muttered, hoping it was low enough so only he could hear, but I was pretty sure both Yngvar and Charlotte heard as well.

Geir hesitated for only a fraction of a moment before putting his hand on my forearm. "I've got your back."

I chuckled and awkwardly patted his arm with my free one. How was I supposed to keep spending time with him, only to have it end in a couple of months?

Our food arrived and the talking quieted as we immersed ourselves in it. The chicken bruschetta looked good—downright tasty, even.

Geir started in happily, and I rolled my cutlery out of the napkin and cut up the first piece. It did taste great, with the herb sauce combatting the dryness of the bread and chicken, as well as the both sweet and bitter taste to the salad.

"So, Charlotte," Geir finally said, breaking the silence that had fallen over us all. "Dad told me about your children, but not really what they do."

"Well, Marlene is nineteen. She's still living at home while she's attending university. She's studying interior design. Kristoffer is fourteen and still in primary schooling. He doesn't know what he wants to do yet, but he's got a few years to figure it out still." Charlotte smiled softly. "I hear you're studying arts. Do you know what kind of direction you want to go with it? I think you and Marlene might get on, she's very creative too."

"I don't know what I want to do yet." Geir shrugged. "That's why I'm taking a year of general studies. That way I can go to university too, if I'd like. I hope to figure it out during the next year, though, or else I don't know what I'm going to do next autumn."

"I'm sure you'll find your niche. It'll come to you. Marlene took three years of general studies because she didn't know what she'd like to do. She finally figured out that interior design would be a good career path for her during her last year, right before the application deadline." Charlotte turned to me then, and my anxiety, which had dropped a couple of notches while Geir held the conversation going, skyrocketed. "What do you do, Jørgen?"

"I'm an electrician."

"Is that something you always knew you wanted to be?" Her eyes were trained on me, and she seemed genuinely interested in hearing the answer.

I'd never aspired to be anything. All I'd ever wanted was to be left alone, to not be the victim anymore. "Not really. It just kind of happened. I'm good with numbers, and that particular vocational study had the most maths. I enjoy it, though, so I suppose I chose correctly."

"That's the success to every job, isn't it? To enjoy what you're doing." She took another bite of food thoughtfully. "I've been working off-shore for a couple of years now, which is where I met Yngvar. I do enjoy it, but it keeps me away from home and my children a lot, so that's why I've decided to go back to what I studied. I'm a solicitor, and that means regular hours and evenings spent at home. I hope it won't be too much of a transition for you, Geir." She turned her attention back to him, to my relief. "To be surrounded by a lot of people all of a sudden."

Geir looked startled by her actually acknowledging the impending move. We hadn't talked about it much since that day his dad had broken the news to him, and I didn't think he'd talked to his dad about it much either.

"Umm, no, I don't think so. I guess it'll be nice." I could tell he was a bit dubious about it, though.

He wasn't happy about the move, which was mostly why we didn't talk about it, because it ruined both our moods. I wanted our last couple of months together to be good, not something I'd look back on with sadness.

I suspected he did as well.

Charlotte must've picked up on his sudden change of mood too, because her expression shifted to a more compassionate one. "I know this must be difficult for you. It's not fun to move so far away at the best of times, especially not when you have someone special."

She glanced at me, and I quickly dropped my eyes to stare at my half-eaten meal.

"But it's only for a year. When it's over, you'll be eighteen and then you can do whatever you want. A year might seem a long time now, when you're so young, but it's really not. A lot can happen in a year, too. We're all excited for you to move in, Marlene, Kristoffer, and I. Kristoffer, especially, is excited about the prospect of a dog. They've never had a dog before, because we've never had the time for it."

"Charo is very well behaved," Geir mumbled.

"He's old, though, so he doesn't like to play anymore."

"No matter what he's like, he's welcome." Charlotte was all smiles again. "I own a house, left to me by my parents when they died. It's quite big and spacious, so we won't be crowded. You'll have your own room you can retreat to if we're too much for you. We can be a bit loud at times, and I can imagine you're used to a quiet life. You can decorate it anyway you want, too, though I'm sure Marlene will have several comments and suggestions for you."

"Th-thanks." Geir fumbled with his fork.

I smiled to myself. He was going to have a great year, with a real family who would care for and about him. He wouldn't be spending his evenings alone with only Charo for company anymore.

Things would be better for him now, even if he was leaving me.

I would survive. I was used to not having anything for myself.

I'd thought... Well, it wasn't going to happen now. I wouldn't cut him off, not yet. I would spend the last two months with him, and after that... I'd be alone again.

Story of my life.

CHAPTER 18

 y mobile started chiming in my pocket.

I took a last swallow of my water bottle before I fished it out of my work trousers.

It was Geir. He never rang me.

If we communicated when we weren't together, it usually happened by text. Especially when I was at work.

I glanced at Tarjei, who was sitting next to me eating his lunch. He raised his eyebrows at me. "Aren't you going to get that?"

I slid the bar to accept the call and put the phone to my ear. "Hello?"

"Jørgen." His voice was hoarse, accompanied by sniffles.

"What's the matter? What's wrong?" My blood ran cold at the anguish in his voice.

"It's Ch-Charo!" Geir broke down in sobs.

"What's wrong with him?"

"I don't k-know! He won't get u-up. He won't eat or drink. He's just l-lying on the bathroom floor. I think he's really s-sick!"

"I'll be right there."

Tarjei frowned. "Everything all right?"

I shook my head. "I have to go. Tell the boss it's an emergency."

"Will do. If anyone's allowed to have them, it's you." He made a shooing motion with his hand. "Go. I can handle the job alone. Get off with you."

I stalked off to my car and sped out of the parking space, heading towards Geir's house. His dad had left to go back to work a week ago, after staying home through the entirety of Easter. Charlotte had stayed for half of the three weeks Yngvar was home.

They'd spent Easter at the cabin Yngvar and his brother owned, and though Geir had asked me to come, I'd declined. I had to work on the days that weren't bank holidays.

Besides, I wasn't fit for sleepovers. I struggled in my own familiar bed; I couldn't push myself to stay in a strange one, with unfamiliar people around me wherever I turned.

I parked my car on the kerb right outside their gate and rushed inside the house to the bathroom upstairs.

I stopped in the doorway to take in the scene in front of me. Geir was on his knees next to Charo's head. A bowl of water and a bowl of food were set down in front of him, untouched. Charo was lying on his side, with his head in Geir's lap. His eyes were halfway closed and his breathing was shallow.

Geir looked up at me, eyes red and filled with tears. "I don't know what to do."

He looked so young and lost in that moment, sitting there with his beloved dog and best friend.

"We'll take him to the veterinary clinic." I crossed the threshold and bent down. I slid one arm under Charo's head, the other behind his legs and lifted him up.

He was a full-grown Labrador, and he weighed as much, but I managed to carry him down the steep stairs safely.

Geir hurried after me. He pulled on his jacket and shoes with jerky movements.

He opened the door for me so I could carry Charo outside, his hand shaking as he locked the door. Then he hurried down the path to open the backdoor of my car. I followed and gently laid Charo down across the seat.

Geir walked around and got into the back so he could put Charo's head on his lap again. His fingers, still shaking, slid through Charo's soft fur lovingly.

I closed the door and got into the driver's seat. I sped just as much now as I'd had when I'd driven from work, maybe even faster. I could only hope we wouldn't meet a police car on our way.

Luck was with me, though, because we arrived at the veterinarian's ten minutes later.

I went around the car to carry Charo, and Geir closed the door after me. His tears were dried up for the moment, but he trembled slightly. I could tell he feared the worst.

Honestly, so did I. Charo didn't look good at all. His head lolled against my arm. He didn't seem to have any strength left in him.

The woman behind the counter looked up politely when the doors *whooshed* open, but she hurried around when she realised we were there in an emergency.

"What happened?" she demanded, curt and professional as she lifted Charo's head off my arm to look into his eyes.

"I don't kn-know," Geir stuttered. He stood slightly behind me to give the woman space to examine Charo's head. "I f-found him like this when I got home from s-school. He wasn't his usual self this morning either, didn't really want to go for a proper walk. I just thought he was t-tired, so I gave him food and water and headed off to school."

She nodded. "Come with me." She led us into an examination room where she put a blanket atop the examination table and motioned for me to put him down. "I'll go inform the veterinarian. She'll be in shortly to look at him."

I nodded. "Thank you."

She left the room and the door clicked shut after her.

Geir stepped up to the examination table and bent over Charo, nuzzling his head. "You're such a good boy," he whispered. "Please be all right. Please let there be something they can do for you. You're my best friend, I can't lose you."

His words tore me up inside. Charo was an old dog. I didn't hold out hope that there was anything they *could* do. And if there was, how much longer would he have left to live?

The door clicked open again, and I turned around slowly. A woman, possibly in her early to mid-thirties, stepped into the room. Her expression was serious, but also compassionate.

"Hi, I'm Anne. I'll be examining your dog." She held out her hand to me and I shook it.

"It— it's really *his* dog." I motioned to Geir,

who'd straightened up by now. He still had his hand on Charo's head though, stroking gently.

"Hi, I'm Anne." She shook Geir's free hand. It seemed awkward, with them having to use their left hands, since Geir's right one was on Charo. "Would you like to stay while I examine him? You're free to wait outside if you wish so."

I looked at Geir.

This was his choice.

He swallowed heavily but squared his shoulders. "We'll stay."

She nodded, then went over to look at Charo. "What is his name?"

"Charo."

"How old is he?"

"He's eleven." Geir choked up at that. Maybe he'd come to the same conclusion as I had.

I stepped over to him and put a hand on his shoulder, hoping it would be of some comfort.

She nodded, then started examining Charo properly.

Geir turned his head to look up at me, and I could clearly see the sorrow, the despair, the desperate need for this to go well on his face.

I wanted it to go well too, but I had a strong feeling that it wouldn't. I didn't want Geir to lose his best friend, his companion. I didn't want Charo to die, because I'd come to care for him too, just like I'd come to care for Geir.

"Has Charo been with you long? Does he have a history of disease?"

"He's been with me ever since he was a puppy. There's never been anything wrong with him. He's always been healthy." Geir's left hand came up to squeeze mine. I squeezed back. "He's had all his injections and everything."

Geir turned back to me. It was like he didn't want to see her examine Charo. He probably didn't, but he still wanted to be there for Charo.

Geir was Charo's human, there was no one in the world more important to Charo than Geir was.

"What am I going to do if this doesn't end well?" Geir's bottom lip trembled. He was fighting tears again. "Who's going to assist me when I have a seizure if Charo's not there?"

"I don't know." I shook my head sadly.

"He's a seizure response dog?" Anne asked.

"Yeah, he's trained to assist me when I have a seizure and go for help." Geir swallowed furiously now.

I wanted to draw him in close to me, but I refrained. Partially because we weren't alone in the room, and partially because I was afraid that would make him break down in tears again.

It took a while, with Anne doing a full check-up on Charo and drawing blood. Geir was turned towards me the entire time, but his hand never left Charo's head. My hand, in turn, never left Geir's shoulders. I tried to keep my attention on him, but I couldn't help but glance over at Anne whenever I saw her move out of the corner of her eye.

When she finally stepped back from the examination table I turned my full attention on her. She frowned, but masked it before turning towards us. I closed my eyes briefly as I prepared myself for what was coming.

"I am so sorry," she said, glancing at me and Geir. "He is an old dog and nature is taking its course. It looks to be organ failure, which is a common thing to happen in old dogs. His extremities are getting chilly, which is a sure sign that the end is near. He's dying. I would recommend you euthanise him, as a natural death can take from hours to days. It's easier if he simply goes to sleep and never wakes up again."

Geir didn't say anything, simply stared at her.

For a moment I was afraid he was experiencing an aura, but then I could feel him start to tremble under my hand.

"I will leave you to discuss it." She nodded and quietly left the room.

"Geir."

I finally drew him into a hug, and he came willingly. His fingers gripped at my jacket as he buried his face against my collarbone.

"Geir…"

And just like that, he broke down.

GEIR SNIFFLED, but the tears had dried up. His hands shook, but he did manage to get his signature on paper. He'd opted to stay in the exam room with Charo when he was put down, and I stayed with him for support.

Once he handed the form off to the vet technician, he bent back over Charo to stroke and pet him and whisper to him.

Charo lay there, lethargic and weak.

Anne shaved a small part of Charo's leg, where she'd insert the needle. "Are you ready?"

I could see how Geir closed his eyes for a couple of seconds at the question. When he opened them again, he nodded.

"Remember, you need to hold him down firmly.

Once it's been injected, it'll only take seconds to put him to sleep."

Geir nodded again. "Yeah."

He didn't look when she injected the needle. He kept his focus firmly on Charo.

Anne was right; he fell asleep in seconds. She listened to his heart with a stethoscope, then sighed and put it away. "He's gone."

Geir didn't react. He kept petting Charo.

"Geir." I stepped up behind him. "Come on. He's gone."

"No." Geir moved away from me and buried his face in Charo's neck. "He can't be. No."

"I'm sorry." I didn't know what to do for him. I had no idea. I'd never experienced anything like this before. I'd experienced death of someone close to me, but my uncle's had been a relief, and Kay... Kay's had been hard. But it had been his choice, and I liked to believe he was happier dead.

He was at peace, something he'd never been when he'd been alive.

Geir's shoulders shook.

I put both my hands on his shoulders now, squeezing. "I know this is hard for you." Maybe I shouldn't have said anything, or touched him, because now the sobs set in full-force.

He clutched at the lifeless dog, refusing to let go.

I had no idea what was expected of me. What was I supposed to do? I was completely lost. I didn't have experience with this kind of grief, not when it came to other people.

I grieved Kay, of course, but that was on me. There wasn't another person who'd cared about him like I did. I'd become even more withdrawn as a consequence.

But Geir was a completely different person than I was, and I had no clue what he needed of me.

"I will give you some time to yourself," Anne said to me with a glance Geir's way. "I'll let you say a proper goodbye."

"Thank you."

She slipped out of the room, and now Geir's sobs were the only sound I could hear.

How many times had I cried like that, but for a completely different reason? When I'd been locked in the basement or been curled up in my bed after one of my uncle's nightly visits. When I'd been huddled in the bathtub holding the knife to my skin because I couldn't see any other way out.

How many times had I seen Kay curled up on his bathroom floor, sobbing exactly like Geir was now? Too many times to count.

But I had never, not once, lost someone as dear to me as Charo was to Geir.

So I stood there, having no idea what to do while Geir sobbed and clutched at his dog.

The sobs quieted down after a while, and his grip on Charo's fur loosened. When he finally lifted his head, his skin was red and blotchy and his eyes were sore looking.

He turned to me, and it was then I could finally see the lost look in his eyes.

"What am I supposed to do now?"

I shook my head. "I don't know." How could I know what he was supposed to do? I couldn't know that. I didn't even know what to with myself, so I certainly couldn't tell anyone else what *they* were supposed to do.

Geir drew in a shaky breath. His eyes filled up with tears again.

"I can't ever remember being without him. Mum and Dad got him for me when I started my second year in school. He's been there for me through every-thing. Through Mum's death, through every seizure I had at home, he's been there with me every night, every day. What am I going to do now without him?"

I was about to suggest getting a new dog, but I stopped myself in time. It would definitely *not* be the right thing to say. Besides, a new dog could never replace the old one anyway, could it?

"I don't know."

He buried his head in his hands. I finally manned up and walked over to him, wrapping him in my arms. "I'm sorry," I whispered against his hair, my voice thick. "I'm so sorry."

After a while he pulled away from me and turned to Charo. "I love you, Charo. You've been my best friend for most of my life. I love you so much!" He couldn't speak after that as the tears started streaming again.

I slid my arm around his shoulders and gently steered him out of the room.

Anne stood at the counter with the receptionist who'd greeted us. They both looked at Geir with compassionate, sad expressions.

Anne came around to face us properly. "I am so sorry for your loss."

Geir swallowed and cleared his voice. "W-when can I get his a-ashes?"

I stepped up to the counter while Anne spoke to Geir.

"I'm sorry," the lady said quietly. "It's always sad when you have to put a pet down."

"Yeah." I nodded slightly. I took my debit card out of my wallet. "I'm going to pay for him."

Geir shouldn't have to pay for deciding to put Charo down. He was already broken over the loss, and having him pay for the injection that had literally killed his dog was not something I wanted him to do.

The price was high, but veterinarians had to earn a living too. The injection, and the cremation, the urn… I paid gladly so Geir wouldn't have to do it.

I got a receipt, which I put in my wallet with my card. After I thanked the receptionist and Anne, I led Geir back out to my car. I opened the passenger door and gently pushed him inside. He all but fell into the seat, the tears still streaming.

I didn't know what to say to him, so I didn't say anything.

I simply drove home.

He got out of the car once I parked, but he stood there staring at my front door with a faraway, lost look in his eyes.

I wrapped my arm around him again and together we went up to my flat. He curled up on the sofa, and I stood over him, uncertain.

"Can I get you anything?" I asked.

He shook his head, then seemed to change his mind. "M-maybe water?"

He drank greedily when I gave it to him. After all the crying and sobbing he'd been doing, he must have been hungry as well. "Do you want dinner? I could go out and buy us something. Fish and chips, maybe?"

He looked dubious. "I don't think I can eat anything."

"You need nourishment. You need to eat."

He glanced up at me. "Okay. You're right. Yeah." He put his glass on the table and rubbed at his face. "Do you want me to come with you?"

"No, just stay here and rest." I leaned down to press a soft kiss against his forehead. "Don't do anything stupid."

He blinked up at me with wide, red eyes. "Wha—what would I do? Jørgen, I would never..." He moved his head from side to side. "I just—I wouldn't. Who has—I mean, who's—"

I looked down at my feet. I hadn't meant to say what I did; it had simply slipped out. I knew he wasn't the type to do anything drastic. He'd been living with bullying and loneliness all his life. Even if he'd lost the one closest to him, I didn't for a second believe it would break him.

Geir was strong.

He was sad now, of course he was, his dog had just died, but he'd live through it and he'd come out stronger.

"I'm sorry, I didn't mean to say that. I don't mean to imply that I think you'd do something. I don't think you will. Really, I don't."

He took my hands in his. "Who has? Jørgen, answer me. Who has?"

"My uncle shot himself," I said to my feet. "And my friend, Kay, jumped from the bridge. You know, *the* bridge where most people who commit suicide by jumping in this town does it from."

I hadn't been a witness to my uncle's death. For a man who'd made my entire life hell up till then, he'd decided to spare me of the sight of him shooting his brains out.

Talking about Kay, though… I'd stopped going to my therapist around the same time I'd met him, and it had all been downhill from there. The therapist in question had helped on that point, too.

"If you want to talk about it all, Jørgen, you know I'll listen." Geir's voice was low, still hoarse from all the crying, but it was soothing.

"I don't." I shook my head. "I—I can't." It was like a block in my mind. A block that had chipped slowly through the years, but it was still there and intact and I was slowly drowning thanks to it, and I just couldn't. Couldn't talk, couldn't *think* about it.

Geir was already heartbroken, and if I said as much as a single word more I would suffer a complete breakdown. I couldn't let that happen. I needed to care for him now, and I had work in the morning.

I pulled away from him. "I'll go buy dinner."

He didn't say anything, but I could feel his eyes on my back as I stalked to the door.

Maybe it was a good thing he was moving away from me and my mess of a life.

CHAPTER 19

I woke that night to a slight shaking of the mattress.

Considering how much I struggled with sleep when there was anyone in bed with me, it was a wonder I'd even fallen asleep at all.

I turned my head to my side and encountered Geir's T-shirt-clad back. His shoulders shook. He was crying again.

"Hey." I rolled over to wrap my arm around his waist.

"I'm sorry. I didn't want to wake you, I really tried to be quiet."

"It's okay. I don't want to sleep when you're sad, anyway." I tightened my grip. He put one hand on my bare upper arm, gripping tightly. "You don't have to feel sorry at all. If you need comfort, all you have to do is ask, you know. You don't even have to ask, you can just roll over."

"I was a-afraid to startle you. I didn't want you to have a f-flashback or a panic attack."

"Do you want to talk?" I know I'd refused to talk earlier, but my kind of issues weren't something I could just talk about in a sitting.

"I keep thinking about him being gone. And tomorrow… Tomorrow's May seventeenth. What if it had happened then, instead of today? He would've been suffering all day, since everything's closed. So I'm thinking it's good that it happened today, and then I feel guilty because I think that, because I don't want him to be dead."

Constitution Day. That hadn't even crossed my mind.

If he hadn't mentioned it I would've shown up at work tomorrow only to find it closed.

"Don't feel bad about that. You don't want him to suffer, so it happening today was… not good, of course, but more convenient. I'm sorry, I don't know what I'm saying."

He chuckled. "I get where you're going. I do. Still. He's gone and it hurts *so much*."

"I know."

"Do you have any plans tomorrow?"

"No. Why?" I rested my cheek against his soft blond hair.

"No plans with family?"

I snorted. "No." I hadn't seen any of my family in... months. Besides meeting Christina outside the shop, I hadn't seen or spoken to any of them since Christmas. I wouldn't even have seen them at Christmas if it hadn't been for my Uncle Thomas' persistence and my grandma's arrival.

Grandma never would've tolerated me spending Christmas alone, not when she was there. She was a quiet, timid woman, but she was strict about Christmas being family time.

Thomas didn't want me to spend big holidays alone either, but he didn't push much.

Grandma lived in Spain, though, had for years now, but she tended to come back to spend Christmas with the family. Thomas and the kids, that was, not my dad. My dad was never present in the family, but that didn't make it any easier for me to be around the rest of them, especially not when Jo was there.

"Do you? Have plans with your family, I mean?"

"We tend to spend it together. If Dad's here we're all together, if he's working I go over to my uncle's. I don't want to tomorrow, though. I'd much rather just spend the day here, with you." He sniffled. "I don't want to go outside. I don't want to celebrate. I don't particularly care for the parades either."

"Me neither." A day like Constitution Day was not for me. Too many people, too much noise, too much of everything.

I couldn't handle it. It was too easy to be touched. Staying inside was the best bet for me.

"I'd like to spend the day with you. Beats spending it alone."

"I want to spend every day with you," he whispered in a thick voice. "It's only a little over a month left."

I tensed up. He was right. School let out at the end of June, so we didn't have much time left. I didn't want to think about it, so I turned my face to bury it in the back of his neck.

He moved his hand away from my forearm, slipped it under my own, and entwined our fingers.

I squeezed his fingers gently, letting him know it was perfectly okay.

He sighed deeply, sniffled, then settled down.

A month…

The previous months had gone by so fast. Had I started caring about him too fast? He was young, with his whole life ahead of him. He deserved so much more, but he wanted me.

I wasn't about to argue, because I wanted him

too, I wanted to be with him so much my chest hurt for an entirely different reason than it did when I suffered panic attacks.

Still, the fact was that he deserved someone who could give him everything he'd ever want and need.

I didn't think I was that person.

~

"How are we going to do it when I move?"

Geir looked up at me from where he was stretched out on the sofa.

"I don't know." I hadn't ever been in a relationship before—and certainly not a long-distance one.

"We are going to keep in contact, right?" He blinked rapidly as his eyes teared up again. After Charo's death yesterday, everything seemed to make him emotional.

"Of course." I didn't want to let him go. At the same time I didn't know how to hold on when he was so far away.

It wasn't like I could go visit him. Me, down in the capital? It was a recipe for disaster. All the people, the big city, all the noise... No. Just the thought made my skin crawl.

He sat up, then scooted over close to me, fitting himself against my side.

I wrapped an arm around his shoulder.

"We'll text each other, and talk on the phone." He sighed as he put his his head down on my shoulder. "That's all we can do."

Sadly, yes.

"I'm going to miss you," he said, voice low and shaky.

"I'm going to miss you too." I was going to miss him so much.

I was used to having him around now. He was a breath of fresh air in my otherwise solitary life. And now he'd leave it in a month... I didn't like the thought of going back to how my life had been before him.

It was time to change the subject, before I started to cry. "Have you told your uncle you're not celebrating with them today?"

"Yeah, I sent him a text earlier."

"What'd he say to that?" I hadn't met any of his family besides his dad, and considering his dad didn't like me, I had no idea what he'd said about me to his brother.

"That it was too bad, but it was my choice." He buried in closer to me, almost climbing into my lap. "My aunt's made my mum's chocolate cake for me, but... I can't go there. Not now, not today."

Because no matter what, this could never be a happy day for Geir.

Yesterday he'd gone off to school, leaving his best friend home to wait for him, and today... today his best friend was dead.

"It sucks that dogs don't live as long as we do," he muttered against my T-shirt. "Eleven years... It's not really long at all, if you put it into perspective. He's been with me most of my life up till now. What am I going to do on my own?"

I tightened my grip around him, hoping to give him some silent support.

"Dad's forcing me down to Oslo with him, and now I don't even have Charo there to keep me company. It was the only good thing about this whole mess—that at least he'd be with me, even if you aren't." He started to cry softly again. "Now I'll be down there without both of you."

I didn't know what to say.

I was so exceptionally bad at this.

He lifted his head to look at me. Tears made wet tracks down his cheek, but he wasn't sobbing his heart out like he did yesterday. There were only silent tears, there because of grief and because his impending move.

I kissed him, because it was the only thing I *could* do.

His lips tasted faintly of salt after the tears, but they were as soft as they always were.

I tugged him in closer and he tentatively slipped one leg over me, so he now straddled my lap.

It was the closest we'd ever been, except when spooning in bed. I also found I didn't mind, even though he was atop me. He wasn't dangerous to me, after all—except for my heart. It was slowly breaking and I didn't know how to stop it.

"Part of me wish I'd never met you," he admitted once the kiss tapered off. Our lips still rested together, our noses bumping. "Because then I'd probably like the thought of moving away. But the bigger part of me is glad I met you and wouldn't be without these months for anything."

"Yeah…" I felt the same, the same conflicted emotions.

"It's torture knowing that I have to leave soon and not being able to have any say in the matter." He reached up to caress my cheek. "But I wouldn't be without this for anything. These past few months have been the best months of my life."

My breath hitched, and I couldn't find the voice to agree with him. But he was right. What he said was all too true.

The past few months had been the best months of my life too.

In fact, it had been the first time ever I'd truly been happy.

It was a strange feeling, but a good one. That it would end soon, when I'd just had a simple taste of it, was unfair.

But I couldn't say any of it, because that would make him feel even worse. And if it was one thing I didn't want, it was for him to feel worse than he already did.

"Let's enjoy the last month together." I stroked his arms. "As much as we can." With Charo's death, it would be even harder, because Geir was inconsolable after the death of his dog.

I hoped I could be of some help to him during it.

"Yeah." He leaned in again, lips brushing mine in a feather-light kiss. "Let's enjoy the time we have left."

I drew him into a harder, proper kiss.

He melted against me, body moulding to mine.

And for once, I didn't have a negative reaction to any of it. For the first time ever, I could enjoy contact with another human being without being plagued by flashbacks or an instinctive reaction to pull away.

GEIR WAS COMPOSED when he was handed the box

containing the urn. He also got Charo's collar, which he'd forgotten to take off when we'd he'd been put down.

The same veterinarian, Anne, was there to give it to him, but the receptionist was a different lady.

Geir thanked her for her help, and apologised for being a mess, after which she assured him he had nothing to be sorry for.

He was also handed a form that stated the ashes were only Charo's, which he'd been assured would be the case before he'd signed the consent form for the euthanasia.

He held the box close to his chest as I drove him home. He didn't speak, so I didn't either.

I did, however, follow him inside once I'd parked.

We walked into the living room in silence.

Geir opened the box and lifted the small wooden urn out of it.

"To think that this is all that's left of him." He ran his hand over the urn. "This is what he's reduced to."

"At least you have that to remember him by." I wasn't sure it was the right thing to say, but what else could I say? Nothing could make this moment any better for him.

"And this." Geir took the collar up from his pocket. It was simple black leather collar with a tag in front. "He was such a good dog. The best."

He lifted the urn again and put it atop the fire-place. "In films, they always have like a shelf or something atop their fireplace, where they keep urns. I've never seen anyone have that in Norway. It can stand there, though, as long as we're not using the fireplace. He liked to lie in front of it on cold days, when we lit a fire in it. It was warm and relaxing for him."

I wrapped my arms around him from behind. "It's a good place to keep it."

He leaned back against my chest and rested his head against my neck. "I haven't even told Dad yet."

I knew that, because he'd stayed with me ever since Monday, when it'd happened. His Dad had rung him, but Geir hadn't been able to say the words.

So Yngvar was still blissfully ignorant of the fact that their dog was dead.

Someone shouted from the hallway. "Geir? Are you in?" Footsteps came over to the living room, and a man, quite like Yngvar but not exactly, peeked into the room.

His eyebrows drew together as he spotted us standing there, together.

Geir straightened up slightly and I let my hands fall away.

"Uncle?" He wiped at his eyes, even though the tears filling them hadn't fallen yet.

"What's wrong?" The man, the uncle, stepped further into the living room. "Geir? Why are you crying?"

My eyes snapped from the newcomer to Geir, and yes, the tears had started to fall. Must've been him rubbing his eyes that set them off.

"Hey…" I stroked his back in what I hoped came off as comfort.

Geir rubbed furiously at his eyes, but when the tears had first started they weren't about to stop easily.

"Geir." His uncle looked concerned, and he kept glancing at me. I didn't know what he was thinking, if this was my fault or not, but it all made me extremely uncomfortable.

"It's Charo."

"What's wrong with him?"

Geir turned his tear-streaked face towards the urn. His uncle's eyes followed his line of vision slowly, and I could see the moment the truth sank in. "Oh, no. Geir. No." He looked back at Geir, shock and sadness warring on his face.

Geir nodded jerkily.

"When?"

"M-Monday." Geir swallowed heavily and brushed tears off his cheeks. "We've just been to pick up the a-ashes."

"Oh God." The uncle strode over to Geir and scooped him up in a tight hug. I stepped back, uncertain what to do with myself now. "I am so sorry, Geir. Why didn't you tell us before? You could've stayed with us."

"I've been staying with Jørgen."

That brought their attention to me and I fidgeted uncomfortably.

Geir stepped out of his uncle's hug and came over to me, touching my arm softly. "This is my uncle, Daniel. Uncle, this is Jørgen. He's... uh. My boyfriend, I guess." He looked at me as he said it, as if asking for permission.

I guess we were, yeah.

We hadn't talked about being proper boyfriends, only that we'd take it slow. But we spent all our free time together. I'd met his dad and future step-mum. Nothing said *relationship* as firmly as meeting the family.

I shook hands with the uncle, Daniel. "Nice to meet you."

"Nice to meet you too." He was certainly a lot nicer than Yngvar had been.

"Uncle's a psychiatrist."

I blanched, then was instantly embarrassed.

I might have an issue with a certain therapist, but it wasn't Geir's uncle. "I'm sorry."

"Hey." Geir leaned into me. He slid one arm around my waist carefully, as if worried he wasn't allowed to or afraid to. It was probably the last one. My psyche was messed up, after all.

Daniel glanced between us but didn't comment. "How are you doing? Are you doing all right, all things considered?"

Geir nodded.

"If you don't want to stay at home, you know you can always come to us, right?"

Geir nodded again. "I do know that. I just—I'm staying with Jørgen until—you know."

Daniel nodded. "We haven't heard from you in a while, so I thought I'd come over to check on you."

"I sent you a text on the seventeenth. That I was fine, but not celebrating with you."

"You did. Still, we worry about you, you know."

"I know." Geir smiled slightly. "Thanks, Uncle. I really appreciate it." He wiped at his face again. The tears weren't falling that quickly now, but they were still trickling. "We were just coming back here with the urn. I'm staying with Jørgen now."

Daniel nodded, then glanced over at the urn. "Does your dad know? I talked to him last night, but he didn't say anything."

"I haven't told him." Geir got choked up again. "I

don't know how to tell him over the phone. I don't know how to say it period. I—I miss him so much."

"I understand that. Do you want me to tell your dad?"

"Could you?" Geir sniffled.

"Yeah. Of course." Daniel reached out to pat Geir's upper arm. He didn't hug him again, but that could have more to do with the fact that Geir was leaning against me. "I'll tell your dad."

"Thanks, Uncle."

I could tell he was relieved, and so was I, to be honest.

The burden of having to tell his father would now be lifted off his shoulders, and though it didn't make him feel better, it made it a bit easier, at least.

I'd take whatever small favours made this easier for him.

CHAPTER 20

eir showed up on my doorstep on our last night together with an over-night bag thrown over his shoulder.

I let him in with a heavy heart.

"So." He stood in front of me, feet moving uncomfortable. "Tomorrow's the day."

"It is." I took his bag from him and set it down, then drew him into a tight hug.

His arm wrapped around me and his fingers clutched at my shirt.

"What'd your dad say about you spending the night?"

He shrugged. "Don't know. Didn't ask or tell him."

I closed my eyes, but couldn't hide the low laughter his words brought out.

"Don't tell me I'm immature," he muttered. "I'm angry. I've got a right to be."

"Still, he's your dad, he only wants what's best for you." I didn't want Geir to fall out with his father. Their relationship had been strained lately, and though I hadn't seen Yngvar since our lunch before Easter, I heard enough from Geir.

He was *not* happy with his dad. And he didn't have to be. But Yngvar was still his dad, and he clearly loved his son. "You should be glad you have a dad who loves you."

"It doesn't feel like it right now. Like he loves me, I mean." Geir pulled back and wiped his fringe away from his forehead. "He knows how much I don't want to move, and yet he's still barreling forwards with it."

"He's in love." I hadn't got to know Yngvar much from our one lunch together, but it had been obvious he and Charlotte loved each other a lot.

"*I'm* in love," Geir insisted. "But he doesn't care about *that*."

I stilled.

He blushed, but his gaze didn't waver from me. "I am, Jørgen. I'm in love with you. So bloody much."

I drew him into a hug again, unable to speak. I squeezed him tight and he hooked his arms around my waist, leaning into me all pliant.

"I think—me too," I finally managed to force past my lips, whispering it against his hair.

I'd never been in love before, never felt any kind of love or had love directed at me. But what went on inside me now, the swirling of emotions, the sadness at knowing in less than twenty-four hours we'd be separated, and the joy at having him in my arms... if that wasn't love, then I didn't know what was.

We eventually untangled ourselves and moved in the living room.

"So what now?"

I'd wanted to take him out to dinner, at a proper restaurant, for his last night. But I'd had a really bad week and couldn't stomach other people. "I thought we could order take-away?" And get it delivered straight to my door, as well. It was worth the extra money, especially on days like these.

He nodded. "That sounds good."

The evening wasn't at all enjoyable.

I was antsy from my bad week, he was in a dark mood because of his impending move, and... yeah. We couldn't enjoy ourselves.

It wasn't the last night I'd wanted to have with him.

But it was the one we had, so it had to be good enough.

Our final night.

Our goodbye.

I'd wanted it to be special, but I couldn't *do* anything. I couldn't take him out, because there were people everywhere and a flashback and panic attack would ruin everything.

I couldn't do more than kiss and cuddle him, because the simple thought of anything more than that would also lead to flashbacks and panic attacks —and also subsequently ruin the night.

"This is shit," Geir said eventually, like he'd read my mind.

"Yeah." I couldn't do anything but agree, because it was the truth.

He stood up—and my heart nearly stopped beating. "Are you leaving?"

"What?" He stared at me with a funny expression. "No." He came over to stand in front of me, gaze meeting mine. "I'm staying right here." His gaze searched mine for a long minute, then he sat down across my lap. "This is okay, right?"

"Of course it is." I put my hands on his waist.

He slid his arms around my neck, then leant in so we were pressed together. His face buried against my neck, his breath tickling my skin. "I want to stay like this forever."

Yeah. So do I.

But I didn't say it.

Instead I only held him close. It was all I could do. I was too messed up for anything else.

Maybe it's good he's leaving. That he's getting away.

I squeezed my eyes shut and turned my head to press against the top of his.

I never wanted him to leave. But was that selfish of me? I couldn't keep him tied to me and all my mess. He was young, he could get so much more out of life than me and everything I brought to the table.

He shouldn't be with me.

I wasn't fit to be with anyone.

THE DAY HAD COME. The day Geir would leave town.

We'd both had a restless night.

I'd woken up right in a flashback, and feeling the presence of someone else next to me had led me straight into a panic attack. It had taken him forever to coax me out of it, and when I'd finally calmed down I'd had to take a shower and change the sheets.

They'd been drenched in sweat.

Besides my breakdown, Geir hadn't got much

sleep himself. He'd been tossing and turning, miserable about what the morning would bring.

"How was your last day of school?" I asked sometime during the night, when we were both awake and staring at the ceiling.

"Okay." He rolled over onto his side so he faced me. "Nothing happened. Jonas didn't do anything for once. Then again, I was only there for my grades anyway."

"What about your exams? Did they go well?"

"They went okay. I mostly got fours in my classes. Got a five in art, though. And three in maths."

"That's not bad at all." I turned over too, so now we lay face to face. "A three in maths is average. You can't complain about that." I'd graduated with a six, top grade, in maths. But it had also been the only class I'd got a six in.

He made a face. "I wish I could've got that up on a four too. It's dragging my average down. Still, I guess it's okay. And I've got another year of maths left during general studies, so maybe I'll make up for it then."

"I'm sure you will." His fringe had fallen over his eyebrows and I reached out to brush it away.

Please don't leave.

My doubts from earlier had done a complete one-eighty. I wanted to have him in my life, and I wanted him to want to be there. He made me feel better, and maybe with more time I could *get* better too. Maybe I wouldn't be a hindrance… maybe, eventually, I *could* give him all that was expected in a relationship.

Beyond all, I desperately wanted him to stay.

But it wasn't meant to be.

He was leaving, and I drove him over to his house.

It felt like a walk to the gallows. The closer we got to his house, the closer I was to execution.

His dad was already outside, accompanied by his brother. It was warm enough now that jackets weren't needed anymore and both men were in their T-shirts.

I wore a thin, long-sleeved jumper—to hide my scars more than anything. Geir also wore a jumper, but his was tight and he had a T-shirt over it. He kept the sleeves rolled up to his elbows though. His SOS bracelet flashed in the sunshine.

We got out of the car at the same time and met up front.

Geir looked at his dad's car, which was loaded with their most important belongings. When he looked back at me, his eyes were wet.

"I don't want to leave."

"I don't want you to leave, either, but you have to." I stared down into his green eyes.

How much I'd come to care for that specific colour, how much I'd come to care for *him*. I'd never thought I'd ever get to care about someone again, after Kay, but then I'd met Geir.

And now he was being taken away from me.

It wasn't permanent; he could come back.

He *planned* on coming back.

But he might see just what the world had to offer when he'd lived in a big city. I could never be a part of that.

He was young and he needed to live his life.

I, on the other hand, needed to sort mine out.

I reached into my pocket and withdrew a folded paper. "Here." I thrust it into his hand and closed his fingers around it.

He blinked in confusion. "What is it?" He looked at my hand enfolding his.

"It's Nikolai's number. He's Tarjei's little brother and a year older than you. He's moving to Oslo this summer to study at some dance academy. You should ring him up, he's really nice."

I didn't know Nik well, and the thought of him hadn't even crossed my mind before Tarjei mentioned it a couple of days ago.

Geir's eyes filled with more tears as he looked back up at me.

I fought them myself, but I had years of practice, so I managed to hold them at bay.

He threw himself at me, surprising the hell out of me, but I caught him up and held him close. His arms wrapped tight around my neck.

"I'm going to miss you so much," he said against my neck. "Don't you dare shut me out, Jørgen, you hear me? I'm going to ring you, and you're going to answer me, and we're going to keep in contact. I'm coming back for the holidays and I want to be with you then. Every single holiday, you hear me?"

I nodded mutely.

He wanted to come see me every holiday? Autumn, Christmas, winter, Easter... then summer. He'd sworn he would move back next summer.

I dearly hoped he would.

I hoped he wouldn't forget about me and leave me all alone, because I didn't want to be alone anymore.

Not after having known him.

"Jørgen?" He drew back to stare up at me. "You hear me? Don't leave me."

Our last month together hadn't been as we'd hoped. There'd been a lot of tears because of Charo, and now there were even more. It couldn't be helped, though. We'd still had a good time together all in all, even with everything.

I shook my head. "I'm not going to. I won't ever leave you. You're leaving me." I hadn't meant the last part to sound so accusative, but I couldn't help it.

He closed his eyes for a second, which finally prompted the tears to fall. "I'm coming back. I am. You hear me? I'm coming back."

I nodded, but I needed to make one thing clear. "Promise me one thing." I pushed at his shoulders so I could hold him at an arm's length. I needed him to understand.

"Even if you are coming back, next year or in the holidays or whenever... Just promise me that you'll live your life. If you meet someone, go for it." It hurt to say it, but I needed to. "You're seventeen years old, Geir. You're young, you have so much ahead of you, so much you *need*. I can't give that to you. Not now, maybe not ever. So if you meet someone you do want to go further with, do it. Don't think about me."

"Of course I think about you!" he snapped, cheeks reddening. "I want to be with you, so you're the only one I do think about."

"I know." I stroked his shoulders, hoping to calm him down. "And we're together... We'll *be* together. Whenever you come here, it's you and me. But while you're down there, do all the stuff you've never been able to do here. Make friends, go out partying, hook up. Do stuff that normal teenagers do." God, but my chest *hurt*. "I *never* got to do normal stuff when I was a teenager. I could never do anything other people take for granted. I don't want you to miss out on everything I did, okay? I don't want that." My tears started falling during that speech, and I drew in a deep breath at the end, trying to calm myself.

He stared up at me. "Even if I do all that... it'll still be you and me?"

"Yeah." I stepped forward again and bent to press our foreheads together. "You and me. Of course it'll be you and me. Just live your life while you can, that's all I ask. Do all the things I never could."

He gripped at my neck tightly. "Do you believe me when I say I'll come back?"

"For holidays, yeah. But coming back for good... I don't think you will. Not after being away for a year and seeing what there is out there. What do you have here? Nothing."

"I have *you*. That's all I want to have. I don't care about anything else as long as I have you."

"You might feel different in a year." I knew he believed so now, but after living in Oslo, where he would have a family who cared and hopefully friends...

I couldn't hope that he'd be back, because if it didn't happen, it would break me.

He shook his head but didn't deny it. Maybe he

knew there was a possibility that things wouldn't turn out the way he imagined now, or maybe he sensed my need to not hold out hope.

Instead of speaking, he tilted his head to the side slightly and pressed his lips against mine.

We didn't kiss often, which made it all the more special when we actually did. It was probably my fault, being so standoffish, because I was pretty sure he wanted more.

More than I could give.

I wanted to give him more, I wanted to give him everything, but I wasn't able to.

Maybe, in a year... maybe I would have myself sorted out by then.

If he came back.

His lips were soft and tasted salty from his tears. I bet mine did too. It didn't matter—it was *him*. He tasted good no matter what.

He clutched at me once we broke the kiss. "I don't want to go," he whispered. "I don't want to."

"Your dad's waiting." I chanced a brief glance up. Yngvar and his brother were turned towards each other, not looking at us, but the car was ready, the front door closed. I bet it was even locked.

He was leaving *now*, and there was nothing I could do about it besides let him leave.

"You have to go, Geir. He's waiting for you."

Geir shook his head again, but he did start to back away. "I'll ring you, okay?" His voice was thick with emotion. "And you'll answer, right?"

"Of course I will." I'd always answer him, no matter what.

He made to turn around, to head over to his dad's car. He froze, though, turned back, and hurtled towards me.

Our bodies connected at the same time as our lips, and he kissed me with the kind of passion he'd never shown before.

I tried to answer, but I was pretty sure I came up short. Passion... I'd never known passion.

He smiled through his tears when he pulled away. "Autumn holiday, Jørgen. I'll be here. You better be waiting for me."

I nodded mutely, unable to form a word, least of all a sentence.

He walked off and I stood there, staring after him.

He hugged his uncle, waved, then headed down to his dad's car. He stared over at me for a long moment before he finally opened the door and got inside.

His dad shook hands with his brother, then he took his place in the driver's seat. He, too, cast a glance my way, and I thought I saw him nod, but I was frozen. I couldn't nod back.

I watched the car as Yngvar started it and then as it drove down the road. When it signaled and took the turn at the end, it was out of my sight, and it was like the air popped out of my lungs like a balloon.

My feelings that had been carefully kept in check blew up and I collapsed on the ground in front of my car. The tears I'd shed earlier were nothing to the torrent that started up now.

I curled in on myself as the sobs started wracking my body.

He's gone.

The only person I really cared about was *gone*.

It wasn't fair that I always drew the shortest straw. Why couldn't I be happy for once? Why had I been singled out and broken so much that it messed up the rest of my life? Why couldn't anyone have cared about me before it was too late?

I pulled at my hair, needing something to ground myself.

It didn't work. I couldn't calm down. My sobs were getting stronger, hurting me every time they wracked me.

My tears wouldn't stop, even though my eyes burned.

My brain wouldn't stop *thinking*. I wanted it to stop for one bloody *second*—

"Hey, son. Come on."

A pair of hands gripped my shoulders.

I jerked away. I didn't recognise the voice, but that didn't mean much. People who hadn't known me had hurt me too.

"Jørgen. You have to get up, son. Let's have a chat, you and I. Just a friendly chat, nothing more. Maybe with coffee?"

The hands were back on my shoulders and I tried to move away again, but it was difficult when I was curled in on myself like I was.

"Come on, Jørgen. I know it hurts that he's gone. We can talk about it if you want. Or we can chat about something else entirely. It's all up to you."

That voice was soothing.

Not like Geir's was, but it was kind and comforting and it didn't sound like it would hurt me.

I slowly let go of my hair and straightened up. I looked up into kind green eyes. They were almost the same shade as Geir's, but not quite.

"Up you go." He grabbed my arm and helped me up on my feet. I had to bend over once I was on my feet, as my chest constricted and it *hurt*.

"Get in the car, son. I'll drive us." He opened the passenger door for me, and I fell into the seat.

I leaned forward and buried my face in my hands. They shook, but so did the rest of me.

The driver's side door opened and a person sat down heavily in the seat next to me.

He turned the keys that I'd left in the ignition, and drove away from the front of Geir's house.

Geir's old house.

"I think it's time you get some help, Jørgen," Daniel said.

ABOUT THE AUTHOR

TT lives in Norway and writes about gay men living in Norway. She also occasionally writes about gay men living in the UK, because she loves the UK. Norway might be too cold for her, but TT doesn't like the summer, so she's learned to adapt. TT is happiest in front of her computer, creating emotional stories about men loving other men.

www.ttkove.com
ttkove@gmail.com